Dare to Rock

THE DARE TO LOVE SERIES, BOOK #5

NEW YORK TIMES BESTSELLING AUTHOR

CARLY PHILLIPS

SPENCER
HILL
PRESS

Dare to Rock
Copyright © 2015 by Karen Drogin

Please visit www.carlyphillips.com

First Edition: 2015
Carly Phillips

Dare to Rock: a novel / by Carly Phillips—1st ed.
Library of Congress Cataloging-in-Publication Data available upon request

Summary: Avery Dare lives a quiet life in Miami as an online fashion/makeup
video blogger. She has good friends, a close, large family, and if her love life
is lacking, she likes it that way. But when she receives an invitation to one of
her ex's concerts, along with an invitation to meet him backstage, she decides
to take the risk . . . and comes face-to-face with the reality of his rock star
lifestyle—the press, the crowds, and the half-naked groupies.

At eighteen, Grey Kingston left everything he knew and loved behind to
seek fame and fortune as a rock star, and he found it as the lead guitarist and
singer for the band Tangled Royal. Yet at the height of his career, he's ready
to walk away and return home to a simpler life . . . and the woman he left
behind, if he can convince her to give him another chance. Except moving on
isn't as easy as Grey would like. And Avery isn't sure she wants the pressures
that are part of Grey's life . . . but she doesn't want to lose him again either.
Can their recently renewed love survive the fallout?

Published in the United States by Spencer Hill Press
This is a Spencer Hill Contemporary Romance.
Spencer Hill Contemporary is an imprint of Spencer Hill Press.
For more information on our titles visit www.spencerhillpress.com

Distributed by Midpoint Trade Books
www.midpointtrade.com

Cover design by: Sara Eirew
Interior layout by: Scribe Inc.

ISBN: 978-1-63392-087-3
Printed in the United States of America

The Dare to Love Series and NY Dares Series

Dare to Love Series
Book 1: *Dare to Love* (Ian & Riley)
Book 2: *Dare to Desire* (Alex & Madison)
Book 3: *Dare to Touch* (Olivia & Dylan)
Book 4: *Dare to Hold* (Scott & Meg)
Book 5: *Dare to Rock* (Avery & Grey)
Book 6: *Dare to Take* (Tyler & Ella)

NY Dares Series
Book 1: *Dare to Surrender* (Gabe & Isabelle)
Book 2: *Dare to Submit* (Decklan & Amanda)
Book 3: *Dare to Seduce* (Max & Lucy)

The NY Dares books are more erotic/hotter books.

CONTENTS

Prologue

Sweat poured off Greyson Kingston's body, and his heart beat a too-rapid rhythm, the high and the adrenaline rush from his performance still pulsing through his veins as he walked into the lounge backstage. He pulled off his soaked shirt and tossed it onto the floor, grateful for the stocked room and waiting pile of towels. He grabbed one and dried his face and hair, deliberately trying to slow his breathing.

The sound of Tangled Royal fans stomping their feet and demanding an encore echoed through the walls, but the band had performed their final song. Even as his pulse still soared.

He glanced toward the door. "Did she pick up the ticket?" Grey asked Simon Colson, their manager, who was busy texting on his phone.

"What? Who?" Simon, ever the well-dressed Brit, shoved his phone into his trouser pocket. No jeans for him. "Good show," he said to Grey and the rest of the band, ignoring Grey's question.

Lola Corbin, their lead singer and Grey's best friend, was still bouncing in her heels, not yet coming down from their shared high either. "We did rock it," she said, tossing her dark hair over her shoulder.

Milo Davis, their bassist, grunted something and fell into a chair in the corner. Grey narrowed his gaze. Milo barely had the energy for a full concert these days, and that worried him.

But right now, Grey had bigger concerns and turned to Simon. "I asked you if Avery Dare picked up the VIP tickets I told you to leave at the box office."

Simon shrugged. "I couldn't tell you."

Grey scowled at his manager's *I don't give a shit* tone. More and more lately, Simon's lack of consideration for what the band members wanted grated on Grey's nerves. Lola might be considering using him for her solo career, but anything Grey did going forward wouldn't be with the man.

At least he'd indicated he had left the tickets. He'd be out of a job if he screwed with Grey on this. "Fucking find out."

"What's so special about this piece of ass?" Simon barely got the words out because Grey grabbed him by his collared shirt and pinned him up against the wall.

"Talk about her like that again and you're done."

"Whoa." Lola put her petite body between them, pushing Grey away from their manager. "Everyone breathe," she muttered. "You. Go take a walk and calm down before your company shows up," she ordered Grey.

He stormed off, missing whatever lecture she gave to Simon next.

Though the man had done his job well, helping maneuver Tangled Royal to the elusive top of the charts, he cared about the bottom line and not much else. Especially not the fact that Tangled Royal was more than a band, that they were also people with real feelings, issues, and lives. No wonder Simon didn't believe how serious both Grey and Lola were about changing their futures.

Danny Bills, their drummer, already had a wife and two daughters who lived in LA. He was ready for home time, and everyone knew it. Milo was another story. If he didn't stop the drugs, he wouldn't have a future.

As for Grey, he hoped for more than the travel and fame that had been so important to him way back when. He hoped for *her*.

His eyes flickered to the door. No sign of Avery. He tipped his head back, wondering if she'd come backstage or ignore the invitation . . . and him. His stomach gripped painfully at the thought of not seeing her again. She was the one person who not only understood the loner musician he'd been as a teen but grounded him when he'd threatened to spiral. With her soft voice, that thick mane of dark hair, and those indigo-like eyes, she'd burrowed someplace deep inside him. Still, she hadn't been enough to hold him, not when fame, fortune, and the need to be something *more* lived within him.

But it was Avery whose face he saw in the nameless women he'd fucked over the years. Avery whose belief in him kept him going when times were hard. Funny how that worked. He wondered if she'd thought of him over the years and if she was hyped up about possibly seeing him again now.

A loud scream brought him out of his thoughts. He glanced up as a group of women poured into the room. Half-dressed, teased hair, too much makeup, and enough perfume to make him gag. Fucking Simon never listened. Grey had specifically told him not to let any of their crazed female fans backstage.

Grey pushed himself off the wall and stormed over to his manager. "I told you no more groupies after concerts." Especially not tonight, when he was expecting Avery.

He shot a disgusted look at the women fawning over a dazed Milo. They wouldn't give a shit if he were dead; they'd want a piece of him anyway. The thought made him want to gag.

"Wasn't me. Security obviously didn't get the message," Simon said, but Grey wasn't buying it. Simon always had an agenda.

"Grey!" one of the woman shrieked, her high pitch nearly piercing his eardrums.

He glanced up just as one of the groupies he recognized threw herself at him, wrapping her arms around his neck. Her big fake tits pressed uncomfortably against his chest, and she raked her clawed nails through his scalp.

"Baby, you were so good! So hot onstage. I just knew you were singing directly to me."

He choked over her sickly sweet scent. More because he'd been dumb enough to screw her once, years ago, after a concert and way too much to drink. She'd been trailing after him ever since. He attempted to detangle himself from her, but she wasn't letting go. *This* was why it was time to call it quits.

"Marco!" Grey called out for the bodyguard who usually prevented him from being mauled, but the guy was nowhere to be found.

Beside him, Simon merely grinned, pleased with the fact that the band was liked, wanted, and making him money.

"Back off," Grey said to the woman, pulling at her arms, but she had them locked tight around him.

"Baby, you don't mean that."

"Oh, I really fucking do." He glanced over, hoping to catch Lola or Danny's attention and get help when his gaze fell on the woman who had just entered the room.

She was so beautiful she took his breath away. Wholesome yet sexy, creamy skin, gorgeous, silky dark hair, and a nervous expression on her face as she looked around, her overall appearance in stark contrast to the harsher-looking groupies who followed the band.

And she hadn't seen him yet.

Left with no choice, he was going to have to physically extricate himself from the clinging octopus of a woman. He grasped her around the waist, intending to push hard, just as Avery's gaze landed on him, her eyes flickering from his to the woman he *looked* like he was holding in his arms.

A flash of emotion flickered across her expressive face. Everything from awareness and shock to disgust and hurt all showed on it before she swung around and headed for the door.

"Avery!" He called her name loudly enough to be heard across the room while shoving the groupie, sending her tripping backward.

She wailed and began crying, and her friends surrounded her, but Grey ignored her in favor of Avery. He reached the door just as Avery paused and turned to him.

"Avery." His gaze met hers.

She blinked, a mix of pain and confusion in her unique lavender-colored eyes. "I shouldn't have come."

"Yes, you should have." She was so close he could see the light sprinkling of freckles on the bridge of her nose, and his heart threatened to pound out of his chest. "This isn't what it looks like."

She tipped her head to one side. "But it *is* your life. The one you worked hard to achieve and . . . I'm happy for you." But the words were at odds with the sad smile lifting her glossed lips. "It's good to see you, Grey." She raised a hand his way before she turned and walked out.

Shit. "Avery!" He stepped into the hall.

"Kingston!" Simon barked out. "I've got *Rolling Stone* on the phone, and they want an interview. I need an answer now."

A glance back told Grey that Avery had gotten lost in the crowd held back by security. His head pounding, he walked back into the lounge, ignoring his manager.

"Was that her?" Lola came up beside him, her voice soothing in light of the chaos swirling around him.

"'Was' is the right word," he muttered. "I can't do this anymore, Lo."

She laid her head on his shoulder in commiseration. "I hear you. It's not good for us either. Rep doesn't like the crap that comes with this lifestyle," she said of her serious boyfriend, who was the Miami Thunder's successful wide receiver. "I want to be around during his upcoming season, and he worries about me when we're on the road and he can't be there." She let out a huge sigh. "We do have a tour to finish though."

"We do," he agreed. "But afterward? I'm coming home." And he was going to get his girl.

Chapter One

Five Months Later

"And always remember to be your best self!" Avery waved at the computer screen and hit the stop button on the recording. Another video *in the can*, she thought wryly. She'd rewatch later and do her editing before putting this one in the queue with the others.

She taped ahead, and she felt good about the upcoming weeks' worth of material. In between videos, she interspersed her blog with written stories and photos of clothing and makeup and the celebrities who wore them well. Those she also wrote ahead of time. And she had plenty of future ideas, she thought, glancing at the yet-to-be-organized piles of free product that had been sent to her for testing.

One of the perks of being a professional blogger and vlogger with a huge online social media presence: she received packages from companies looking for her to pimp their goods. She also relied on her personal favorite products and looks, for which she did online tutorials. It'd begun as a cool hobby, but she'd somehow turned it into a career, and she loved it. She supported herself, supplemented by a trust fund courtesy of her maternal grandparents. She was lucky and she knew it. She never took her life for granted.

The irony of her online persona, when compared to her real-life one, never failed to amuse her. She was far from the extrovert she portrayed herself to be. When she was nine, she'd experienced her first panic attack after the scandal had broken about her father's second family. The paparazzi had wanted more information about her family, and they hadn't been above targeting a child to do it. She still had nightmares about the flashing camera lights and the crushing hordes of people coming at her. That incident and the ensuing ones had caused her to withdraw, preferring the comfort of friends and family to large crowds and intrusive strangers.

With those closest to her, she was comfortable and outgoing. To Avery, vlogging was still the equivalent of being behind the scenes, and she had no problem portraying that side of herself on camera. She provided her viewers with advice and how-to instructions on wearing the newest fashions and current makeup styles. She was twenty-five and played to her age group and younger, and her perky persona worked, making her a success. As a result, her fans looked at her as their *friend*, someone to whom they could relate.

Her brother Ian might be president of the Miami Thunder football team and her father the owner of a renowned hotel chain, but Avery never flaunted her family name or wealth. She'd had enough public scrutiny to last her a lifetime, and she never sought attention outside her small channel on the Internet.

A familiar *ding* alerted her to incoming e-mails, and she clicked back to her mail program. An e-mail notice from a local gossip blog caught her eye, and she read the subject.

Reports of Tangled Royal breakup confirmed.

Avery bit down on her lower lip, not surprised by the mention of the band but always dismayed by the accompanying painful twist of her stomach.

Grey Kingston, Tangled Royal's lead male singer and guitarist, had been Avery's high school boyfriend and first love. And up until five months ago, she hadn't heard from him in seven years. Then one day, a letter had arrived from Grey, telling her he was leaving her concert tickets and backstage passes. He'd ended with, *Love to see you again. G.*

After a lot of consideration, because Avery always thought things through, she'd gathered her courage, invited her sister, Olivia, and decided to attend. Memories of that night still haunted her.

She wasn't naïve or stupid. She understood the magnitude of the kind of life a rock star like Grey Kingston led. Even if she hadn't known, she'd been force-fed pictures and snippets of information over the years by the same online sites she read to keep her blog current. And she'd be a liar if she didn't admit to setting a Google Alert to Tangled Royal and buying their albums and listening to them in secret, where her family and friends wouldn't know or judge her. But the on-screen photos and gossip columns had nothing on what she'd seen with her own eyes.

She'd walked into the room to find a half-naked, bleached blonde wrapped around Grey like a second skin. The other female fans in the room had been dressed equally skanky, and they'd surrounded the band members, serving to remind Avery of how different she and Grey's lifestyles were. And how they each had always wanted opposite things.

She'd left the VIP room before she and Grey could do much more than look into each other's eyes. A long, history-filled stare that threatened all the defenses she'd built up against him after he'd left town . . . and left her behind. One look at the handsome face she used to love had hit her hard, and she'd known then and there that she would need to protect herself. And she was right.

Grey hadn't given up. Every time she posted something meaningful on her blog, like a hot new handbag or a delicious-smelling perfume she'd sampled and adored, the same product ended up being sent to her doorstep, gift-wrapped beautifully, with a short card attached.

I'm sorry —G

Give me another chance —G

Can't wait to see you —G

Missed you all these years —G

Yeah, that last one got to her most. Because she'd missed him too.

Then, as routinely as the presents had arrived, they'd stopped. He had sent a note telling her he'd call when he was back in town, but that had been weeks ago, and she'd stopped holding her breath. No doubt he'd decided she wasn't worth the effort, not when he had all those easy conquests and female groupies at his disposal.

She'd tried to put him out of her mind, not all that successfully. Now this band breakup notice stared back at her from the screen. Her finger hovered over the keyboard before she finally gave in and opened the e-mail alert and read the article in its entirety.

Grey Kingston has been sighted in and around Miami and South Beach over the last week while bassist Danny Bills has been settling into LA, adding fuel to the rumors that the band is going their separate ways.

So Grey was back in Miami and had been for a week. So much for his promise to contact her when he returned to town, she thought, her chest tightening not with her familiar anxiety but with true pain.

Though she knew she shouldn't be all that surprised. It was just another letdown by another important man in her life.

This one had once stolen her heart. Only recently had she come to realize she'd never truly gotten it back.

"Hey." Ella, her roommate and best friend, stood in the doorway of Avery's bedroom.

Avery pushed her chair back and forced a smile. She'd met Ella Shaw when they were both at Miami Children's Hospital, donating bone marrow. Avery was nine; Ella had just turned ten. They'd bonded, shared summer and holiday visits, and claimed each other as best friends. When Avery's sister, Olivia, had moved out and married Dylan Rhodes, Ella had moved in.

"You okay?" Ella asked.

"I am awesome," Avery said, turning her back on the screen and alert, grateful a photo of Grey hadn't accompanied the message. She didn't need to see his handsome face on her screen. Bad enough he occupied so much of her thoughts.

Ella plopped down on Avery's bed, curling her legs beneath her. Her damp, light-brown hair hung around her face in silky strands. "And I don't believe you." She pinned Avery with a knowing stare.

"Okay, I'm not awesome." Avery had never been able to lie to Ella, not since the day they'd met.

On top of Avery being easy to read, Ella had an intuitive sense, in addition to her warm, giving personality, and Avery adored her. Meeting Ella was one of the good things that had come of that painful time in Avery's life.

"I'm guessing Grey Kingston has something to do with you being distracted and *not awesome*?" Ella asked, making air quotes with her fingers.

Avery pursed her lips and nodded.

Though she hadn't told her family what had happened when she'd gone to see Grey backstage, it was obvious to them all she'd been upset and not herself afterward. But she had confided in Ella. It wasn't that Avery didn't want to tell her sister, but the time had never been right. Olivia's life had been in upheaval. First, Dylan's old friend Meg had been in the hospital, and they'd been busy with her troubles. Afterward,

Olivia's life had fallen into place. She and Dylan were in love, and Avery hadn't wanted to burden her sister with her own issues.

"Still no word from him?" Ella asked, bringing Avery back to thinking about Grey.

"No. And I shouldn't care. I mean, I'm the one who told him to stop texting me and to focus on his tour." Avery settled herself on the edge of her bed.

"And you only told him to leave you alone because you're scared to start something with him again. Besides, it's not like he listened to you." She gestured to one of the many gifts he'd sent . . . and she'd placed around her room.

"But he did say he'd be in touch the next time he was in Miami." Avery picked at a nonexistent piece of lint on her silk pants.

"And?" Ella pushed, never allowing Avery to escape into herself as she was prone to do.

She swallowed over the surprisingly painful lump in her throat. "I just read he's been back in town for the last week or so."

"And he still hasn't been in touch."

"No. And I shouldn't care! I don't want to care."

"But you do." Ella patted the space beside her.

Avery crawled up the mattress and curled against her pillows. "I'm being ridiculous. I should be relieved he's forgotten about me. I saw him with those groupies, and I ran from everything his lifestyle represents, didn't I?"

"You did," Ella agreed.

"So why do I care that he decided I'm not worth it?"

"That's not what he decided!" Ella exclaimed, shaking her head in frustration. "If I could wrap my hands around your father's neck for all the insecurities he caused you, I would."

Insecurities was probably an understatement, Avery thought. And truly, only her sister, mother, and brothers could completely relate to the belittlement they'd felt on discovering their father's betrayal. They'd always believed their hotel magnate father, Robert Dare, was away from home, traveling extensively on business. And he'd always made up for what he didn't provide in time and presence with gifts.

They'd thought he worked hard to support their family and had accepted his absence as routine. Until the day he'd informed their mother, Emma, that he had not only a mistress but another three children on the side. And one of those children—the youngest, Sienna—needed a bone marrow transplant in order to live, and he wanted his legitimate kids tested as potential donors. Bless her mother, she'd always been kind and caring and, despite her own pain, had agreed.

Avery had been the match, the child her father had used to save one in the family he'd devoted his time to. The family he clearly loved more than Avery's. To say she'd felt used and abandoned was an understatement of extreme magnitude.

Ella pulled her in for a brief hug. "I've known you for a long time, and you've told me things your siblings don't even know, right?"

Avery nodded. Ella had always been her safe place. Grey had too . . . once. She pushed the thought aside.

"Then trust me when I tell you that you can't let the feelings of inadequacy your dad left you with rule your life. I know it didn't help when Grey left you to find fame and fortune, and you've convinced yourself you're not enough, not worthy. I'm here to remind you that you are."

At her friend's true and telling words, Avery trembled. As hard as she'd tried to overcome it all, some days, the inadequate feelings came rushing back.

Ella grasped Avery's hands. "Mr. Tangled Royal would be lucky to have you in his life. Not the other way around."

Avery blew out a deep breath, replaying her friend's words in her mind. They helped. "You're right. Dealing with Grey after all this time has made me feel like I've been abandoned all over again. Except it's not the same. And I've moved on."

Ella eyed her with amusement. "Now, I don't know if I'd go that far."

Avery smacked her with the nearest pillow, and her friend laughed.

"But I would go so far as to say you've grown up a lot since you two saw each other last. With a little luck, so has he."

Avery rolled her eyes. "Ever the optimist?"

Ella shrugged. "Can't hurt to think positively, right? So if he does get in touch and he wants to see you, I think you owe it to yourself to meet up with him. Think closure, if nothing else."

"When did you get so smart?" Avery asked.

"The day you became my best friend. Remember, it's easy to give advice to someone else about their love life."

As open as Ella was with most things, she didn't talk much about her own guy situation. She claimed there wasn't anything to discuss, which made no sense, because Ella was pretty, sweet, and she outshined everyone around her. She deserved a great man in her life.

"Anything *you* want to talk about?" Avery asked, hoping that for once her friend would open up.

"Nope. I actually have to get to work. I promised my boss I'd meet with a new photographer she's considering hiring." Ella was an assistant to an up-and-coming fashion designer based out of Miami. Another reason they were such good friends—they shared a love of clothes, makeup, and design.

"Okay, well, thanks for the talk," Avery said.

"Anytime." Ella pushed herself off the bed just as Avery's cell rang from across the room.

"Toss me the phone before you go?"

Ella grabbed the phone from beside the computer and squealed as she handed Avery the cell. "Looks like Mr. Tangled Royal surfaced."

Avery's eyes opened wide as she stared at Grey's name on the screen.

"I want all the details later," Ella called out with glee before heading out of the room.

Grey sat in his apartment, surrounded by warm cream-colored walls and the soft brown-and-taupe furniture Rep had left behind. They had similar taste, and the place already felt like home, giving Grey the comfort and sense of peace he'd missed while being on the road. His gut told him the other part of home lay in reconnecting with Avery.

He'd begun the process toward the end of Tangled Royal's tour, sending her a steady stream of gifts corresponding to the things she mentioned on her blog, smartly named *Avery's Attitude.* He wished he could take credit for being so creatively brilliant, but it had been Lola's idea, as a way to get back into Avery's good graces.

The first gift and card he'd sent had contained his private cell, and he'd asked her to text him. She had. Which had started a stilted and hesitant back-and-forth dialogue between them. Lola had been right—the gifts were a good opening gambit, and he'd kept them up . . . until Milo had OD'd, and everything in the band's life had screeched to a halt as they'd tried to help their friend.

The early days of rehab hadn't been easy. Milo had threatened to leave more than once, Lola had cried, Grey had begged and done everything short of taking his best friend's place to get him to stick it out. By then, the band had fulfilled their concert commitments.

The timing made sense. Lola had cemented her relationship with Rep and decided to buy a place on secluded, private Star Island. Grey, in turn, had put in motion the process of buying out both Lola's and Rep's condo leases downtown. The board had finally approved his application, speeding things up because of his interest in the two apartments on the same floor. Lola's side he intended to turn into a soundproof studio.

All of which had occupied his time. Not to the exclusion of Avery. She'd never been far from his mind, but everything he did had been methodically planned out. He wanted to be

settled before approaching her again. If they had any chance
of seeing what could be in the future, she had to believe the
life he desired now wasn't the one he'd left her for once
before. Or the one she'd seen backstage.

He picked up his cell, dialed her number, and listened as it
rang and rang. All the while, he was hoping he hadn't blown
his second chance with her before it ever began.

He was preparing himself to leave a message on voice
mail when suddenly she picked up. Relief swamped him, and
Avery's soft, dulcet tones settled something deep in his bones.
"Hey, sugar," he said, suddenly nervous about what to say.

"Grey, this is a surprise." She sounded distant. Cool.

"I told you I'd call when I got to town."

But she obviously hadn't believed him, and now he knew
just how much of an uphill road he had ahead of him. Good
thing he wasn't afraid of working for what he wanted.

She cleared her throat. "So when did you get back?"

He bent his knee and settled into the sofa. "I've been back
for a little over a week. I wanted . . ." He trailed off, at a loss.
Fuck. "I'd rather fill you in in person."

She hesitated and then said, "I'm really not sure it's a
good idea."

He glanced heavenward, praying for an opportunity. Something he could work with. "Give me a chance to just talk to
you. If, after that, you don't even want to be friends, I'll back
off." He was lying through his teeth, but that was okay.

All he wanted, needed, was for them to spend time together
and both experience their old chemistry. He trusted in their
long-ago connection. Thinking of her had gotten him through
many lonely times. He refused to believe that bond was gone.
He wanted to feel it again and needed her to see that what
they'd shared as teenagers could be even more solid as adults.

The silence on the other end of the phone nearly killed
him, but he let it go on. Though it wasn't his nature to let life
dictate to him, he sensed she needed the illusion of control.
He'd start by not pressuring her.

"Okay, we can get together," she finally agreed.

He released a long breath. "I already made a reservation at Tino's," he said, knowing she'd recognize the restaurant. "Saturday night, if you're free."

"Pretty sure of yourself," she muttered.

"Pretty hopeful," he corrected her. "Can you make it?"

She hesitated before answering. "Yes."

He refrained from pumping his fist in the air.

"What time?" she asked.

"Eight."

"That works. I'll meet you there," she said in an obvious attempt to keep things short and distant.

That wouldn't work for him. "I'll pick you up at seven thirty."

"Grey—"

"Avery—" he mimicked, like he used to every time she'd tried to argue with him.

Her light laughter eased the heavy weight on his chest.

"Fine," she said, giving in. "I already know you don't need my address." Her tone softened at the unspoken reminder of the many gifts he'd sent over.

"No, I don't. I'll see you at seven thirty on Saturday. And Avery?"

"Hmm?"

"I can't wait to see you," he said, hanging up before she could answer . . . or worse, not say the same.

Chapter Two

On Saturday night, Avery tried on four outfits, finding something to criticize about each and annoyed with herself for caring so much about impressing Grey. But the fact was it had been years since she'd seen her ex up close and personal, and she wanted to make an impact. She wouldn't be a normal woman if she didn't.

Finally, she decided on a bohemian-looking dress, baby-doll style with kimono-draped sleeves in a variegated array of blues, accented by her favorite silver necklace. She slipped on silver gladiator sandals and styled her recently highlighted hair in loose waves. A spritz of her favorite perfume, the new one with vanilla and amber undertones that Grey had sent her, and she was ready to go with—she glanced at her watch—no time to spare.

Just as she finished, the doorbell rang. She drew in a deep breath and headed to answer it, grateful Ella was at a business dinner with her boss and a designer who was in town for the weekend. Avery didn't need her friend watching her first interaction with Grey in seven years. She was nervous enough without an audience.

She opened the door and stared at the man standing in front of her. When she'd seen him at the venue, she'd barely had time for a long look, not when he'd had a groupie clinging to him, and prior to that, the last time they'd been together, they'd both been kids.

The guy standing before her was all grown up.

He braced a hand against the frame and grinned at her. "Hey, Very," he said, using the nickname he used to call her.

"Hi," she managed to answer, taking in his hotness as she realized the years of seeing him on magazines and the Internet hadn't begun to capture the changes time had wrought.

His features were the same but more mature. He'd grown into himself in a really good way. His jet-black hair was cropped short at the sides, a little longer on top, the rocker-like style suiting him more than the shaggy look he'd preferred when they were younger. She used to run her fingers through the long strands of his hair when they made love. She swallowed the pained sound that threatened to escape her throat along with the memory.

Instead she refocused on him. He was still lean, his faded jeans hugging his body, but now he was well built too. Muscles defined his forearms, and his pecs protruded from beneath his fitted black T-shirt, while drool-worthy tattoos wrapped around his skin, emphasizing those same muscles. The urge to trace the ink in his flesh, to feel the heat and bulk of those muscles overcame her, and she curled her hands to prevent herself from acting on the crazy impulse.

His body was powerful, and she understood how he had the stamina to sing, play his guitar, and grace the stage, running from one end to the next while enrapturing the audience. And she'd be a liar if she claimed to be immune to the masculine strength that exuded from him now.

Her gaze traveled up to his face, and she would have apologized for staring, but she caught his green eyes devouring her much as she'd done to him.

"You look fucking gorgeous," he said, a sexy smile on the handsome face that women swooned over.

She pushed the thought of other women . . . *groupies,* aside, reminding herself this was Grey. Her Grey, once upon a time, but those days were over. "Thank you."

"How about a hug for an old friend?" His voice, deep and gravelly, scratched over her already-sensitized nerves in a wholly seductive way.

Her heart dipped, disappointment racing through her at his use of the word *friend*. And she hated herself for the brief reaction. Still, she stepped forward, and before she could prepare herself, he enfolded her in his strong embrace.

His raw masculine scent with only a hint of cologne enveloped her, heightening the sexual awareness she'd promised herself she wouldn't feel. But her body didn't lie. Her nipples tightened, and a coil of need twisted in her belly. He felt familiar . . . yet not, as she hugged him back, noting he was hard everywhere, from his tight stomach to his solid arms. That insane urge to touch him returned, and she eased back before she could feel or do anything else.

"I'll just get my bag and we can go," she said, her voice too raspy, threatening to betray her. She was eager to take them to neutral, public territory.

"Good by me," he said, his gaze never leaving hers.

She locked up her apartment, and he led her to the parking lot. Before she knew it, he paused by a black convertible. A black Aston Martin DB9 convertible.

Avery's mouth dropped open at the sight of the beyond-luxury vehicle. "Holy shit, Grey, is this yours?"

She didn't blink at the unladylike words coming out of her mouth. Her brothers knew and had taught her about cars, and this was a *car*.

A sexy, proud smile lifted his lips, making him look like the much younger Grey she remembered. Boys and their toys, she thought. Although in Grey's case, she understood the fascination. Unlike Avery, who'd grown up with luxury, Grey's past hadn't been nearly as easy, and he'd worked damned hard for every dollar he'd earned as a musician.

"Couldn't resist." He gestured toward the car. "For the last few years, I've been touring so much I didn't bother with a ride." He shrugged. "I figured I owed myself."

He opened the car door for her, and she climbed inside before he joined her from the driver's side. Plush leather surrounded her. Not even her BMW came close to this kind of comfort, and she wriggled her behind into the seat and groaned. "God, it's like heaven."

He slammed his door shut and shot her a dark look. "This is a get-to-know-you-again dinner, right?"

She met his gaze and nodded.

"Then don't fucking purr like a kitten needing to be stroked. A lot of years might have passed, but you still do it for me," he said, his words very much a warning as he turned the ignition on.

Holy crap. She didn't know how to respond to that. The old Grey had been shyer when it came to expressing his feelings. This man was sure of himself in every way, and damned if she didn't find it sexy. Not to mention the huge rush of happiness swirling inside her at the knowledge that she still affected him so strongly . . . even as her brain reminded her to keep him in the friend zone.

"I'd put the top down, but it looks like rain," he said in a calmer tone. "And I remember how much you hate having your hair messed up after you've taken the time to do it right." He grinned at her then, his mood lightened.

He pulled out of the parking lot, the car's motor revving so that everyone within a good mile could hear. He drove to the strip mall where Tino's was located. Some of the shops and restaurants had changed names, others remained the same, but the overall familiarity warmed her. He parked in a fortuitous open spot out front and cut the engine.

"Do the parking gods always smile on you?" she asked.

He grinned. "Sometimes. Others, you have to call ahead."

She shook her head and laughed at his obvious willingness to use his star status to secure parking. For that, she couldn't blame him. Not when he'd be leaving a two-hundred-thousand-dollar car somewhere where it would be in danger of being vandalized. She doubted Tino minded clearing his prized spot out for Grey.

He hopped out of the car and headed to her side, grabbing her door just as she opened it. Before she could walk ahead, he grasped her hand, the familiar gesture taking her off guard as his large hand wrapped around hers. Sparks of awareness prickled her skin at his touch, arousing conflicting feelings—the sweet pleasure at being with him again and a sexual charge she couldn't deny.

"I can't believe you picked Tino's," she murmured.

His deep-green gaze bored into hers. "Do you think I'd forget our first date?"

He'd remembered. Warmth slid through her veins like liquid honey, softening her toward him.

He brushed his knuckles down her cheek, and she shivered, her nipples puckering beneath her dress. "I want you to remember the good things about us. Not just the shit that comes with being part of Tangled Royal."

And with him, but she opted not to mention it now. As they stepped into the restaurant, the scent of garlic brought back really good memories. She'd always loved Tino's and hadn't been back in years. It seemed fitting she returned with Grey.

"Welcome!" Tino walked toward them, a short man with bushy dark hair, now flecked with strands of gray, and the same mustache he'd always sported covering his face. "So good to have you back home." He pulled Grey into a man-hug, then turned his gaze on Avery. "And you! *Bellisima*," he said, kissing both her cheeks.

"Remember, a private table in the back," Grey said to him.

"Not a problem. I didn't tell anyone you were coming in. Of course someone's bound to notice, but hopefully not till you finish your meal. Come." Tino pulled out two menus and gestured for them to follow, turning and walking to the back.

Grey watched Avery, who had an amused smile on her lush pink lips. Lips he couldn't stop staring at. Or wanting to taste.

She followed Tino, and Grey placed a hand on her lower back for a moment before joining her, a step behind. Her flowing dress ended midthigh, her long, tanned legs accentuated by the flow of the material as she walked. She was even more beautiful than he'd remembered.

She'd opened her door, and he'd been struck speechless. His Avery had long dark hair that usually hung straight down her back. This Avery had chunky blonde highlights, a slight fringe of bangs, and her hair fell in soft waves around her beautiful face, her violet-blue eyes large and sparkling. Even when they were teens, her long limbs would tan, but she'd always protect her face with sunscreen. Some things hadn't changed. Too many had.

"Here you go. Privacy," Tino said. "I'll keep the booth behind you free, so that should help."

"You're a good guy," Grey said.

"This from the man who sent my son an acoustic guitar for Christmas? You gained a fan for life," the older man said.

"I didn't do it for that reason. You mentioned he wanted to learn." Grey didn't want to make a big deal out of the gift.

Tino winked at Avery and said, "I'll send a waitress over for drinks."

"You and Tino kept in touch?" Grey heard the surprise and maybe a hint of hurt in her tone, because *they* hadn't.

His stomach cramped at the thought of hurting her, but at the time, he'd had no choice but to get out. Leaving her hadn't been easy, but making something of himself had been necessary. For so many reasons.

"I came back a couple of years after we formed the band. Saw my mom and stepdad and stopped by here. I met Tino's family." He shrugged, trying to make it seem like it was no big deal. "We kept in touch after."

"That's sweet. How is your family?" she asked.

"Good. I had to fight with Mom and Ricardo in order to get them to let me buy them a house in a better neighborhood."

"They're proud people," Avery said, seeming to comprehend.

Grey didn't. He never had understood his parents. Any of them.

His real father had been a true asshole, an academic who'd judged his son, found him lacking, and never let him forget he didn't measure up. When he'd died, Grey'd been twelve. He'd left Susie Kingston with nothing. No insurance, no way of raising her kids, so she'd gotten a job cleaning homes to support them. Eventually she'd remarried Ricardo Mendez, a nice man who'd stepped in as a father figure to Grey and his older sister. But he was employed as a janitor at the high school, and since kids were cruel, that had made Grey's life damned hard.

"Mom wanted to stay in her old house, but eventually they agreed to move to a small house, nothing huge. And they still kept their old jobs." Which Grey also had never understood and still didn't.

"I'm glad you were able to do something for them," she murmured.

"Yeah, me too."

A young waitress came to take their order. She couldn't be more than seventeen and paused at the table, her eyes wide as they lit on Grey.

"Hi." The word came out like a squeak. "Can I get you drinks?" she asked without meeting his gaze, but her hand shook as it hovered over her notepad. Clearly Tino had warned her not to draw attention to who he was.

Grey gestured to Avery. "What do you want to drink?"

"I'll have a Diet Coke."

"Bud Light for me," Grey said, smiling at the girl who'd finally looked at him, trying to put her at ease. "Do you still eat vegetarian pizza?" he asked Avery.

She grinned, obviously pleased by his memory. There was little about her he'd forgotten. "Yes. Please."

"Large pie, half pepperoni, half vegetarian," he said, handing the girl the menus.

She nodded, scribbled on the paper, and rushed away.

"Poor kid. I think she's star struck," Avery said, laughing.

At the sound of her laughter, Grey released the tension he'd felt talking about his family. Her good humor acted like a kick in the groin, tugging on all sorts of memories, many of them involving them sneaking around to find a place to have sex, her soft laughter inflaming his need even back then.

"Tino probably put the fear of God in her to get her not to react." He'd make it up to the girl with a nice tip.

Silence once again descended around them, but Grey was determined to keep things comfortable. *Normal.* He sensed that *normal* was the key to unlocking *his* Avery again.

"So. How did you become a successful YouTube blogger?" he asked, wanting to hear all about her.

She shrugged. "In college, my friends liked how I did makeup, how I dressed. I don't know. Maybe I had an eye from watching television, reading magazines, and paying attention to social media and pop culture. After a while, their friends from home wanted instruction too, so I would do videos and post them to YouTube, and things caught on."

She shrugged as if it were no big deal. "I started running ads on my site, making some money, and retailers started to send me items to test and post my opinion," she said with a grin, her pride in herself obvious.

He was equally proud of her.

She continued to talk some more, and he listened, fascinated by her expressive voice and features, just so damned happy to be here with Avery, alone, with nobody from his other life pulling at him or wanting him to be anything more than who he was. That's what Avery gave him and always had—the same sense of normal he'd run away from. He needed it now. Craved it like he did music.

Like he did her. They might not know one another well anymore, but he sensed the heart and soul of her hadn't changed. The rest, just details, would come. One thing he knew for sure: their physical attraction hadn't waned. If anything, it had grown stronger.

His cock was completely aware of her, the new scent of vanilla that would now fill his car as much as it already had his senses. And this confident, competent woman sitting in front of him was appealing to him in so many ways.

"I didn't plan on it as a career, but I love it," she said.

He braced his arms on the table and leaned across. "I've watched your videos and read your blog. You're amazing."

Her eyes sparkled with satisfaction. "I know you did, because those gifts were handpicked with perfection. Thank you for that."

"Anything for you."

The waitress returned and served their drinks, disappearing again without speaking.

Avery bent down. She pursed her lips around the straw and pulled a long sip of her drink, causing her throat to move up and down. He stared at her slender neck and the long expanse of skin, so enticing. He remembered kissing that soft spot above her collarbone, suckling hard and leaving a mark that she'd had to wear a scarf to cover. Otherwise her brothers would have come and beaten the shit out of him. He'd had that tendency to want to claim her even then.

He laughed at the memory, and her eyes flew to his. "What's so funny?"

He met her gaze and grinned. "Just remembering something."

"What?"

"The hickeys I used to give you, and how hard you'd try to cover them to protect me from your brothers."

She choked on the soda she'd just sipped. "Oh my God!" Her hand flew to her mouth. "Grey!" she said, horrified.

"What?" He attempted to sound innocent. "If you're drawing a blank, I'd be happy to refresh your memory." He wanted to mark her again. In places that were far from her neck, like the sensitive skin on her thigh, right before his tongue swiped her clit.

He clenched his jaw and shut off that train of thought.

Her cheeks had turned a healthy pink at the thought of old hickeys, and she met his gaze, her eyes darkening at the very idea he'd planted in her brain. Good. He wanted her as hot for him as he was for her. But no way was she ready for what he wanted to do to her now. His cock swelled thicker in his jeans. Yep. Nothing had changed in that area.

"Pizza's here," Tino said, bringing out the food himself. The waitress followed with plates and utensils, and then they were alone again.

While they ate, they talked. Grey kept the conversation neutral, telling her about his friends and bandmates, about Milo and his ongoing stint in rehab. She explained how she'd lived with her sister until Olivia had married and Avery's old friend Ella had moved in. Conversation was comfortable and easy, with the occasional hint of sexual awareness thrown in for good measure.

He was doing a good job of convincing her that their chemistry was still intact when word spread that Grey Kingston was *here*.

They were interrupted by people from town who remembered him and fans who wanted autographs, friends from high school, people who knew Grey's parents, an old math teacher . . . the list went on. And though Tino did his best to keep people moving on, Grey knew this came with the territory. It wouldn't matter if he'd chosen a five-star restaurant or Tino's for its memories, the fans would find him.

As much as he resented the intrusion, he understood that these people had made him who he was, given him the fame he'd sought and the money he'd needed to prove himself—to himself and to his long-dead father, Julius, a college professor, who'd convinced him he'd never amount to anything. Unlike Grey's academic brainiac sister, Julia, named after him, of course. Lucky for dear old dad, Julia lived up to the name, though it wasn't her fault Grey had never measured up in their father's eyes.

So although he might want a more normal life now, that didn't negate what fame had meant to him. Still meant.

Despite wanting to be alone with Avery, he had obligations, and so he catered to the fans. He talked, signed autographs, and took the requisite selfie . . . until finally Tino stood on a chair and yelled, "Show's over. Give the man some privacy to be with his lady."

The crowd dispersed slowly, and Grey glanced across the table. Avery sat curled into the corner of the booth, knees up, her sole focus on her phone. He didn't know if she was texting, browsing, or what, but she definitely wasn't happy.

Neither was he.

"Once people get used to the idea that I live here now, shit like this will die down."

She shot him a disbelieving look.

Fuck. He slid from the booth, took out his wallet, and pulled out some bills, tossing them on the table. "Let's go."

"Where?" she asked.

"Somewhere completely private."

From the minute Avery had lost Grey's attention, she'd been ready to leave. Not because she was a child who couldn't share her toy, but because the influx of people into their private dinner had stirred up a mix of emotions. She still hated huge crowds and curled into herself at the thought of being surrounded by strangers—unlike Grey, who thrived on the attention. It didn't matter how well they clicked, how easily they'd reconnected and shared information about their lives, how much she desired him—the chasm between them couldn't be wider.

She vividly remembered walking out of the hospital after she'd donated her bone marrow, her mom tightly holding her hand, her father still inside with Sienna, when the flash of cameras had blinded her.

Emma, why isn't your husband with you?

Emma, is your husband's illegitimate family more important to him than you and your children?

Emma, how does it feel to be cheated on and lied to in such a spectacular fashion?

These days Avery thought of her father as Miami's version of Donald Trump, with a dose of near-bigamy thrown in. Back then, she hadn't been prepared for the media attention. Her mother had tried to push her through the crowd, but it hadn't been easy and had taken a long time. Or it'd felt like it had. By the time they'd reached their car, Avery couldn't breathe. She'd seen spots in front of her eyes, her knees had buckled, and she'd hit the ground hard.

She'd come to in a cold, sterile hospital room, her mom's worried face hovering over hers. The doctors explained she'd had a panic attack. And when she'd returned to school, the incidents had only gotten worse. Preteens were mean on a normal day. Give them a subject like a dad who had a whole other family and things had gotten downright ugly for all the Dare kids.

Even at nine years old, Avery had felt the pain of being the center of attention and being made fun of, and she'd hated it. The panic attacks began to occur more regularly, and she'd had to go see a psychiatrist for help. She had more control of herself these days, but her need for solitude, quiet, and behind-the-scenes interaction had been set.

But Grey? He shone in front of an audience. An audience and groupies he'd always have following him and invading his personal space, and hers, if she chose to be with him.

Could they be friends? Maybe someday, when she didn't look at him and want to jump his bones like the hormonal teenager she used to be. But they couldn't be more, because if she kept spending time with him, she was inevitably going to fall for him again. She knew that already, and they'd only been together for a couple of hours. He was still the warm, fun, likeable guy he'd always been. He remembered things about them she'd have thought he'd put away and forgotten.

And when he looked at her with those dancing green eyes and talked about hickeys, of all things, she still desired him. He had the potential to break her heart worse than the first time, and even though she'd always known his dreams, she'd been shattered when he'd left. She couldn't go through it again. Any of it.

Finally, his arm beneath her elbow, Grey guided her out of Tino's. The humid Miami summer air smacked her in the face when she exited, but the rain had held off, for now. Free from the crush of fans, she breathed easily again.

He unlocked the car and turned to her.

"Grey, I think—"

"Don't say it." His gorgeous green eyes darkened with the clear intent to get his way. "I didn't take you to a nice, expensive restaurant because that's not who we were. It's not who I am now. Tino's was perfect because I wanted to hang out with you and just talk, and we did that. We reconnected."

He ran a frustrated hand through the top of his hair. "I didn't think things through. I shouldn't have taken you out in public with me at all. Not until you're ready."

She'd never be ready, but that wasn't something she planned to say now. He didn't know about the panic attacks she used to suffer from . . . could still occasionally suffer from. She'd been too embarrassed to admit it to him when they were together before, when they were teenagers. Now she was a grown-up. How could she explain that she didn't know if she could deal with them as a couple now because she had issues someone like him could never understand?

He had tried hard tonight, and she didn't want to hurt his feelings or upset him more. "It's fine," she said. "I know who you are. It's not like I was blindsided, you know? It's just the people, the crowds are . . ."

"Isolating. Uncomfortable. I know. I get it, okay?"

She blinked and looked up at him, surprised at the words he'd chosen. "I thought you loved fame. You left here seeking it and—"

"I left here for a lot of reasons, and I hope one day we'll talk about all of them. But as for fame, yeah, I wanted it, and I know how damned lucky I am to have made it to the level I have. That's why I don't turn away from the people who put me there."

"And I'm not asking you to. I wouldn't." But the whole scene made her panicky and even, in some ways, feel *less than*. A feeling she'd had more than enough of in her lifetime, thanks to her father. And also due in part to Grey's sudden departure from her life.

"I need us to go somewhere quiet. Just the two of us," he said, brushing her cheek with his hand.

She wanted to. Oh, how she wanted to, and she tipped her head into his strong touch. "What did you have in mind?"

He pulled out his phone and began to text while she waited. A few seconds passed, then he obviously received a reply. "Lola said we can go to her boat. It's at the marina."

Avery blinked in surprise. She hadn't expected that. "A boat?"

"Yacht," he amended. "She and Rep own one . . . full crew, captain, and everything. She'll clear it with them, and we can head over there now. We'll just sit on the deck and talk."

Avery glanced up at the cloudy sky. Even in the darkness that had finally surrounded them, she knew the covering didn't bode well for good weather. "It's going to rain."

"So we can go below deck. Trust me, it's comfortable."

She had no doubt that it was. These people lived life in a world completely alien to her . . . and that was saying something, given how she thought she'd grown up privileged. But this wasn't just money. It was flashier. Attention getting. Funny how everything came back to that one word. *Attention.*

"I think it's better to call it a night," she said.

He frowned, disappointment, then determination edging his expression. "So you can build up some more walls? Some more misconceptions about who I am now?"

She opened her mouth, then closed it again. He was right. She wanted to be with him, and she didn't like the idea of running away. So their lives were very different, and she couldn't live in his fishbowl world, but they could still catch up. Have this time together.

"Okay," she said before she could change her mind.

Clear approval flashed in his eyes, and his smile broke down the last of her defenses. "Good. Then let's go."

They climbed into his car and drove to the marina, where security in a guardhouse checked them in. Grey parked his car in a private lot. They climbed out, and he led her to the dock, where huge yachts bobbed in the water, gorgeous in look, intimidating in size. A rumble of thunder sounded in the distance, a reminder that a storm was imminent. Or not. In Florida you could never be certain what the weather would be one minute to the next.

With his hand on the small of her back and tremors of awareness rippling through her body, they walked to the end of the dock.

He stopped in front of a white yacht with red trim, *The Lola* written along the side. "This is it."

"Wow," she said, taking in the gorgeous boat. Yacht. Whatever she called it, it was a beauty.

"Yeah. You're going to love the inside of Lola and Rep's baby. I'm not up on terminology, so I'll just say welcome aboard," Grey said as he pulled off his shoes.

She did the same, and soon she found herself on a deck, with beautiful wood furniture topped by cushions with a red-and-white chevron pattern. Lola clearly loved red, she mused.

She glanced around, her gaze coming to rest on a bucket of champagne in ice waiting for them. "They set this up so quickly?"

"Told you. Full-service crew, who you'll never see unless you want to." Grey gestured to a love seat, where they could sit side by side.

She lowered herself into the soft cushion. He joined her, his hard thigh touching hers, and an electrical shock jolted her system. Her body flushed with heat, her nipples tightened, and she bit back a sigh of pleasure. Not quite fast enough, because his eyes darkened at the sound that escaped.

He tore his gaze away, and with expertise, he opened the champagne and poured them each a glass.

"Thanks." She accepted hers, grateful for something to do with her hands.

"To new beginnings." He touched his glass to hers.

"To old friends," she said.

He narrowed his gaze, clearly aware of her attempt to put distance between them. Still watching her, he took a long sip.

She followed suit and moaned at the bubbly taste.

His gaze heated up at the sound, and she just knew a heated blush stained her cheeks. "I always was a sucker for champagne," she murmured.

"I remember. You were a lightweight too."

She shrugged. "I still am." It didn't take much alcohol to give her a buzz.

He placed his glass down on the table in front of them. She preferred to hold onto hers for security. Now that she was alone with him, butterflies had taken up residence in her stomach.

"I needed this. Needed to be alone with you." He reached out and wrapped a section of her hair around his finger and rubbed his thumb back and forth over the strands.

She felt the caress between her thighs, arousal and need alive and well inside her, an ache only Grey seemed capable of creating. "I'm glad we're here too."

"Could have fooled me," he said in a gruff voice. "You tried damned hard to get out of it."

He looked and sounded like a hurt little boy, and she couldn't have that. "My rational side reminds me of how different we are." She met his gaze, needing him to understand. "But I do want this time with you now, to catch up and get to know each other again." But that's all she'd admit to wanting, Avery thought.

"Good, because I want the same thing." He eased closer, his arm snaking around behind her, the closeness and warmth of his body arousing her in a way she hadn't felt in years. Or maybe ever.

He took the glass out of her hands and placed it on the table. "I've moved here for good."

His words took her off guard. "I thought for sure you'd end up back in LA."

He shook his head. "Not happening. I'm here to stay. And since I am, I think we should move on to other things," he said, the sexual innuendo in his tone clear.

"What things?" she asked in a husky tone.

"This." He leaned in and pressed his lips to hers, sliding his tongue over her lips. "Mmm. Champagne and you. Nothing sweeter," he said, his voice a deep rumble, a sweet, seductive promise of things her body craved badly.

Her sex clenched, and she shifted in her seat, unable to ease the sudden ache between her thighs. Her hands drifted as she fought an inner battle—give in to what she wanted or let fear of losing again consume her.

He licked the corner of her mouth and slipped his tongue inside. Battle lost. She moaned, wrapped her arms around his neck, and kissed him back, all the years of pent-up need and longing gone the instant she gave in.

He swept one hand into her hair, wrapping the long strands around his fist, the tug drawing a direct line to her sex. Dampness coated her panties, and her nipples hardened, aching for his touch. But he held her in place, taking his time, his lips devouring hers, his tongue thrusting in and out, sweeping through the deep recesses of her mouth. She was lost in sensation, lost in Grey.

Thunder sounded closer, but at this point, she couldn't distinguish between the arousal rumbling through her brain and body and the weather outside. He kissed his way down her neck, her throat, his teeth grazing her skin, pausing at her collarbone to find the sensitive spot he'd always favored.

She curled her hands into his shirt as her head fell back and she gave into sensation.

"You taste like vanilla," he muttered, licking his way across her chest, following the line of her shirt where it crested over her breasts.

It was the very best kind of tease, and she couldn't do more than sigh his name. "Grey."

"Missed you, sugar."

She trembled in his arms. "I missed you too." The admission hurt, because *he'd* left *her*, and the knowledge was always there, burrowed in her heart, next to the crack her father had left before him.

She pushed the thought away, reaching for him, her hand cupping his cheek. "It's still there, isn't it?" she asked, needing to know the intensity was as strong for him as it was for her.

His darkened gaze met hers, and he stroked her cheek with his knuckles. "Stronger than ever."

He braced her face in his hands and kissed her again—and again it went on, two people relearning and lost in long-forgotten and reawakened sensations. She threaded her fingers into his hair, running her palms over the shorter sides, tugging on the longer pieces on top.

He groaned and pulled her astride him, her sex now in direct contact with the heavy, thick bulge in his jeans. She arched her back and rocked lightly, the cresting waves inside her body as powerful as those surrounding the boat below.

Another crack of thunder sounded, this one louder, startling her, and she flinched at the noise. A streak of lightning lit the sky soon after.

Grey swore. "Inside. Now."

He helped her to her feet. She grabbed the glasses, and he picked up the champagne, but the skies had already opened. Before they could make their way below deck, the first droplet was followed by torrential sheets of rain.

Chapter Three

The sky released unexpected swells of water in seconds. By the time Grey and Avery had made it beneath the overhang and he had led her to the staterooms below, they were drenched.

"Damn. It couldn't have started as light drops?" he asked.

Avery laughed, the sound not helping the hard-on beneath his jeans.

The room had two beds on either side, both of good size for a yacht, and a small dressing area. He opened the closet, grabbed clothes, and tossed two T-shirts onto the bed.

"Pick one," he said, pointing to his old band tees.

"You have clothes on board?" she asked.

He nodded. "Lola insisted I keep things here for emergencies." He looked back in and pulled out a pair of shorts for himself.

"She's a good friend?" Avery asked.

"She is. We met in LA not long after I arrived." He glanced over his shoulder to find Avery had taken off her wet dress. Her bare back with creamy white skin tempted him to touch. Lick. Devour.

He grabbed the other shirt and yanked it over his head, then stripped out of his jeans, trying like hell to ignore the fact that she was undressed inches away. He clenched his jaw and pulled on the shorts, which did nothing to hide his erection.

"Can I ask you a question?" she asked.

"Anything." He spun back to find her seated on one of the beds.

Her damp hair fell over her shoulders, her legs crossed beneath her. But it was his shirt covering her body that had him enthralled. He liked her in his clothing, as caveman as that sounded. He liked thinking of her as *his*.

"You and Lola." Avery picked at a thread on the bedspread. "Have you . . . I mean, did you and Lola ever—"

He paused, then decided he might as well be completely honest. "I never slept with her."

"But you wanted to? Because she's gorgeous. I mean, she was voted sexiest woman alive and all. What guy wouldn't want her?" Avery's cheeks flamed as she rushed out the words. "Never mind. It's none of my business."

"Actually it's very much your business." He strode over to her, bracing his hands on either side of her body, forcing her to lie down on the mattress.

The scent of vanilla and rain permeated his senses, nearly knocking him on his ass as desire rushed through him. He wanted nothing more than to toss her on the bed, strip off her clothes, and bury his cock deep in her wet, willing pussy. That wouldn't happen if she thought he had a thing for Lola. He never had.

Avery stared up at him, eyes wide, waiting for his next move. He could get lost in those eyes. Write songs about the color and how the hue darkened when she was aroused. Damp. Wet for him.

He cleared his throat. "Let's get something clear. I never wanted to sleep with Lola. She had a crush on me, but one kiss cured that. For me, it was like kissing my sister, and for her, she realized her feelings for me were more about comfort and family than sex. So no, Lola doesn't do it for me."

"Oh." Avery's tongue darted out, slicking over her sweet lips.

"You, on the other hand, do. You make me fucking hard every time I lay eyes on you." But he couldn't act on those desires and keep her in his life.

He'd have to win her over slowly. Gain back her trust.

This was too much too soon. He knew it. He drew on all his inner strength, kissed her hard, and pulled her back up until she sat on the bed.

Then he walked to the other side of the small room. "When the rain lightens, we can make a run for the car."

"Sounds good."

"More champagne in the meantime?" he asked, turning back toward her.

She lifted her shoulder, and even that little gesture turned him on.

"No thanks. I think I'm good."

She pushed herself back against the pillows, giving him a flash of pink lace between her thighs. He swallowed a groan and discreetly adjusted himself before settling next to her.

"So tell me more about you and your career. What was LA like?" she asked him.

He rested his head back against the pillows, but the small bed kept them in close proximity. He needed this subject change as a distraction.

He thought back to the early days in California. "LA was a crazy scene. I loved it at first. We played gigs and bars for very little money, hoping for exposure. Eventually Simon, our manager, spotted us, and the insanity started."

She rolled to her side and glanced up at him, clearly interested in his past. "The groupies and women?"

He winced but pushed on. "Yeah. I was eighteen, and everything was new and exciting." He knew that while he'd been young and stupid, enjoying life too much, he'd left her behind and hurt her in the process. "It's not that I didn't miss you . . . I did. I just—"

"You had a dream, Grey. I don't blame you for chasing it." He didn't want her forgiveness, not when he could have, should have, handled leaving better . . . for both of them. But he'd wanted out of his parents' house as much as he'd wanted to play for a living.

He swallowed hard. "I saw you, you know. Everywhere I looked. The women didn't mean anything. It was easy sex, just like the drugs and alcohol were easy. But when I closed my eyes, I pretended they were you."

Her eyes dampened, but he didn't want to hurt her more by dwelling on the past. He'd just wanted her to know he hadn't left and forgotten.

"What changed for you?" she asked.

"Milo got heavier into the drug scene, and things became clearer for me. I realized I loved the music but not the lifestyle."

He laid an arm over his forehead, staring at the ceiling. "Lola and I knew we were done long before we all agreed to call it quits. I reconnected with you . . . or tried to. Then Milo OD'd, and all my focus had to go into being there for him. I didn't mean to stop the gifts or texts, but it was a rough time."

"Grey," she said, her voice a light in the darkness that blanketed him whenever he thought of Milo.

"He's okay. He's still impatient, which is cool. He seems committed to getting better, finally." He held onto that bit of hope for his friend.

"Thank you for telling me." She reached out and touched his forearm, her soft touch a balm for the pain in his soul.

He glanced her way. "I don't share with anyone," he told her. "Even Lola has to pull things out of me . . . but it feels right with you."

"So that hasn't changed either. Our ability to open up and talk to each other." A soft smile lifted her lips.

"Thank God for that." He grinned in return. "So how are your brothers and sister?" he asked, curious about her family.

"Olivia is amazing. Like I told you, she's married to Dylan Rhodes. They both work for the Thunder. She's pregnant and due in a few months. I'm going to be an aunt again!" The excitement in her voice was tangible.

"Again?"

"Yes. Ian has a baby girl. Rainey Noelle. She is the sweetest thing ever . . . except that she has her daddy's stubbornness. And Scott's going to be a dad too. He's with a woman who was already pregnant . . . long story, but they're really happy. Just Tyler's still single. And me." She looked away at that admission, obviously not wanting to get into heavy relationship discussions.

Fine by him. He had a plan to build slowly. As long as she was here, he could live with that. "So your brothers are settling down, huh?"

"Yes, but not mellowing out," she muttered, and he caught the subtle warning in her tone.

"In other words, I'd better watch out?" Her older brothers had always been protective of Avery and Olivia, and clearly that hadn't changed. Grey had a hunch the Dare brothers wouldn't like him coming back into Avery's life.

She nodded, indigo eyes as serious as ever. "I'd steer clear if I were you."

"I'm not worried about your brothers, sugar. If I run into them, I'll deal."

"But—"

He placed a finger over her soft lips. "You're worth it."

Her eyes softened, and she touched his cheek, her gaze warm on his. Desire flitted across her pretty face, her eyes darkening, her breath a short hitch.

His body still beat with awareness from their make-out session on the deck, the memory of her wet heat rocking over his cock still teasing and testing his restraint. He wanted nothing more than to thrust into her hard and fast, *now*. And they were alone on this yacht, nothing stopping them from that kind of reunion. Which meant he was hanging on by a damned thread.

He removed her hand from where she'd been stroking his cheek. "I'm doing my best to be a gentleman." And he had a painful case of blue balls to show for it.

"That's sweet but unnecessary," she all but purred.

He pulled her wrist to his mouth and licked her hammering pulse.

She sucked in a shallow breath, trembling at his touch.

"A little while ago, you were still unsure of me and my life. I'm not going to screw up a second chance by fucking you tonight and dealing with your regrets in the morning." Nobody would believe Grey Kingston was turning down sex.

"I won't have regrets," she whispered, but he could tell she wasn't as sure as she sounded.

"You might."

She opened her mouth to dispute his words and sighed. "You're probably right."

Her words hurt even if he'd already suspected as much.

"So what do you suggest?" she finally asked.

He blew out a long, frustrated stream of air and pulled himself together. "More get-to-know-you dates. More making out—but not tonight, on this bed, when you're wearing nothing but my shirt and barely there panties I want to rip off with my teeth."

"Oh my God." She visibly shook at his pronouncement, her nipples hardening beneath the faded T-shirt.

"Yep. Now you understand." He swung his legs over the bed and rose to his feet. "Let's see if the rain's let up."

"Good idea," she said in a trembling voice.

He walked out of the room and climbed up top, relieved to find the rain had slowed to a drizzle.

"We can head back to the car," he said as he returned.

"Good." She held her wet dress in one hand.

He left his jeans and shirt on board. He'd pick them up tomorrow. "What are you doing next Thursday?" he asked, unwilling to take her home without making plans to see her again.

"During the day I volunteer at the Miami Children's Hospital with cancer patients."

He turned to her and stared.

"What?" she asked.

"You amaze me, that's all."

Grey hadn't known Avery when she'd donated bone marrow. He'd entered her life in high school. But she'd confided in him just how difficult that year and those afterward had been, with both the revelation that her father had another family he spent more time with than hers and the fact that he'd needed her or one of her full siblings to donate in order to save one of his other kids. Avery had been the best match, leaving her feeling used and hurt. Yet here she was, years later, donating her free time to help other children who were in her half sister's position.

God, she was something else.

"It's nothing huge," she said, deflecting. "I bring my iPad and makeup. I look through online magazines and sites with the girls and teach them how to feel better about themselves while they're going through treatment."

"That's cool. It really is."

She smiled at him, and it fucking lit him up inside.

"How about afterward? Want to meet Rep and Lola? They invited me over, and I know they'd love to meet you too. No groupies," he promised her before she could find that as a reason to say no. "Just some good friends hanging out."

"Okay."

He blinked. "Just like that?"

She studied him for a long while. "Just like that."

Avery spent Sunday doing laundry, cleaning the apartment, food shopping with Ella, and trying not to think about her feelings for Grey. She wanted distance from his hands on her body, his lips on hers before she could put things in perspective. And since Ella had so much to tell her about her job and the dinner with the up-and-coming designer, Avery managed not to daydream. Too much.

Of course, Ella wanted details about Avery's weekend, and she had to fill those in too. Still, she survived Sunday, and she woke up Monday knowing she had a full day's worth of things to do to keep her busy. Before she could leave the apartment, she had to check her blog and answer messages. Another way to keep her mind off of Grey Kingston.

Except today's blog extolled the virtues of her favorite NARS blush, and wouldn't you know, it was called Orgasm. The well-known product had held a place on most *Best Of* lists in major magazines since the mid-2000s and was a cult classic worth mentioning yearly. But today, it merely served to remind her that she had spent the night alone on a yacht with her gorgeous ex, and she hadn't had one.

Nope, not an orgasm to be found for Avery, because Grey had decided to play it safe. At this point, Avery believed she might be thinking more clearly today if he hadn't held back. If he'd let them both give in to the simmering sexual desire that was so obviously between them. But he hadn't. And she admired his restraint.

It also scared her, because she'd been wearing nothing but his shirt and barely there panties that he, quote, *wanted to rip off with his teeth*. Her entire body trembled at the memory of his words. Her sex clenched, empty and needy. If he'd been able to walk away from that desire, he had a wholly different agenda . . . and she didn't know if she'd survive whatever it was.

He wasn't the easygoing Grey she remembered. He was more dominant in his speech, more frank about what he wanted. And that kiss? He'd controlled it and her, until she'd have done anything just to get more of him. But as much as she wanted him, as much as they had in common, she still believed there were too many differences to overcome.

She had a half a week before she had to worry about dealing with him again, and so she settled in front of the computer to work. On Orgasm.

She answered some reader questions, going back over the weekend's posts, before turning to today's blog. She pulled up the comments and began to read, startled and annoyed to find troll comments under a variety of different screen names. Words like *skank* and *whore* greeted her, and she immediately deleted them, hoping she'd discovered them before too many viewers had seen them too.

She didn't let them get to her. The Internet was full of mean-spirited people who took pleasure in bashing people under the guise of anonymity. She put the insults out of her mind and focused on discussing why the shimmery peach-colored blush worked on so many different skin tones, as well as answering the typical jokes about the product's name in good humor.

Before she signed off for the morning, she refreshed the screen one more time to see if she had anything else to answer. The troll comments had returned, coming in heavier than before, this time adding names she wouldn't repeat out loud alone, never mind in public.

So bizarre. And annoying.

She groaned and called her web people, knowing she needed to have them lock things down before the ugliness spread. They had to shut down comments for the day. And the whole mess took up the better part of her morning, forcing her to reschedule a nail appointment with a new salon she had hoped to feature in one of her posts on local businesses. Finally, she finished with the web hosting company and hung up the phone, praying they'd fix the site before the end of the day.

She headed over to an outdoor café for lunch to meet her sister, Olivia; her sister-in-law, Riley; and her soon-to-be sister-in-law, Meg. When she arrived, the others were already at a table beneath a large umbrella.

"I'm so sorry I'm late!" Avery said, pausing to give each woman a hug and a kiss before settling into the empty seat between Riley and Olivia.

"Relax," Olivia said. "It's fine. Nobody has to rush back to work."

"Yep, summer for a teacher means time off," Meg, a pretty and very pregnant brunette, said with a relieved smile.

"I've been working fewer and fewer hours," Riley admitted. "I really love being home with Rainey." She shrugged at the admission.

Avery grinned. "Your little girl is a handful."

Her sister-in-law pulled her long curls behind her and laughed. "Blame your brother for that part of her personality."

"And you?" Avery glanced at Olivia. "Don't you have a job to do?"

"I can take time to be with my favorite people if I want." She patted her large belly. "It's amazing how the men in the office will tiptoe around a deliberately whiny pregnant woman and give in to anything she asks for." Olivia grinned.

"You have no shame," Avery muttered.

"Nope."

"Can I get you a drink?" a waiter asked Avery.

She glanced around the table. The girls already had their beverages. "I'll have an iced tea, please."

"So how was everyone's weekend?" Olivia asked.

They went around the table, taking turns with their stories. Avery was grateful for the time to get her head on straight and decide what, if anything, she'd tell the women closest to her about Grey. After so many years of wondering about him and missing him, actually being with him this past Saturday night had been surreal.

Her emotions had fluctuated all evening. She'd been wary at first, withdrawn during the influx of fans, then once they were truly alone, all her old feelings for him had swamped her full force. They meshed on a level she'd never experienced with anyone else. He understood the girl she was deep down inside, respecting what he knew of her insecurities. Any other guy would have responded to her blatant sexual overtures and taken advantage of the obvious chemistry and desire pulsing between them.

Not Grey. He wouldn't let proximity and need dictate his actions. Instead of making use of the bed, instead of taking their kisses to the next level, instead of peeling off the T-shirt he'd lent her and sinking deep inside her willing body, he'd called a halt. Because he knew, even if she'd been well past caring, that if they'd had sex, she'd regret it the next day.

And she would have. Of course, she regretted not sleeping with him too, but that was her needy body talking. She'd returned home from the boat on edge, her panties damp, her nipples hard and aching, wishing he'd at least taken the edge off with a nice climax. But instead, her rocker had played the good guy. And she hadn't been able to use her vibrator to slake her need, because she'd known it wouldn't have been as good as the real thing.

"Avery Dare, where the heck are you?" Riley asked, waving a hand in front of her face and bringing her back to the present.

"You're flushed," Meg noted with a grin.

"We live in Miami, and it's hot out," Avery muttered, grasping for an excuse.

"No, that's not a weather flush. It's a guy blush," Riley said, eyeing her with curiosity.

Olivia pursed her lips. "You've been in your own head ever since the concert with Grey, and I've let you stew because you seemed to need time. But you seem lighter now . . . and I want answers." Her sister nailed her with a determined expression that had Avery shifting uncomfortably in her chair.

"Maybe she doesn't want to discuss things in public," the ever-diplomatic Meg said, taking a sip of her iced tea.

Avery realized her drink had been put down, and she took a long sip of the cool, sweet liquid. Olivia was right. She'd been sad and grumpy after her run-in with Grey and his groupie at the concert, and she hadn't let her sister in. She didn't want to hurt Meg's or Riley's feelings by blocking them out now, even if discussing her love life wasn't something she did easily.

"I saw Grey this past weekend," she admitted, then sat back and let the comments fly.

"I can't believe you and Grey Kingston. Damn, girl, he's hot." Meg fanned herself with her hand.

Riley's smile started slow and built until she was grinning. "It's about time."

And then there was Olivia. "You've been holding out on me."

Guilt slid through Avery, and she grasped her sister's hand. "I'm sorry. It's just that after the concert—"

"I don't know what happened after," Olivia reminded her.

Avery sighed. "Nobody does." Except Ella, but Avery wouldn't dig the wound deeper by saying so. "I went backstage, and there was a female wrapped around him. A half-dressed groupie with teased hair and too much makeup, clinging to him like a howler monkey. And yes, he pushed her off him, but then she began shrieking like he'd hit her. She made a scene. He ignored her, ran after me, but it . . . hurt."

"Aww, honey," Meg murmured.

"He knew you were coming and couldn't keep them away?" Olivia asked, outraged on Avery's behalf.

She swallowed hard. "It's part of his lifestyle. That's what had me so thrown afterward. To even be friends with him now, I'd have to expose myself to that, and I didn't know if I could handle it."

"And you couldn't share that with *me?*" Liv asked, really and truly hurt. "I know what you went through because of Dad. I was there for you."

"And I knew you'd be there for me again. But you were busy making things right with Dylan. And then when you did, you were happy. I didn't want my problems to drag you down. Plus you'd have felt bad about moving out, and I didn't want that either. You finally had your happiness, and I wasn't going to let anything stand in the way of that."

"What about your happiness?" Olivia asked, obviously moving on from the personal issues between them.

Avery shrugged. "I don't know. We still click. It's all still there between us, but so are the differences. I sat in a corner for thirty minutes while he signed autographs and took selfies, and that was at a local restaurant."

"You don't think you can handle the spotlight?" Meg asked.

Olivia nodded. "When Dad came clean about the others, and then Avery was a match for Sienna, everything became public. And ugly. Dad's well-known in Miami. It hit the papers, and we had a really hard time in school. From the youngest"—she glanced at Avery—"to Ian, the oldest, kids were awful. Mean. People looked at Mom in the grocery store, whispered behind our backs."

Avery knew Olivia was leaving out the rest to protect her, but she didn't mind confiding in her friends. "I started getting panic attacks after the first time the photographers surrounded us. They yelled horrible, intrusive questions at my mom, and light bulbs flashed at me . . . I was nine. And I freaked out."

"Passed out is more like it," Olivia said.

Avery dug her fingernails into her hands at the reminder. "Yeah. So I really don't like being the center of attention . . . not for any reason."

"Yet you put yourself out on the blog. That's so interesting," Meg, the teacher, said.

"I know. I've given it a lot of thought, and I studied psych in college. Extroverts like Grey feed off the crowd. They get energy and a high from it. For introverts like me, it's draining. I control the blog, I put myself out there on my terms, and the rest is behind the scenes, where I'm most comfortable."

"Makes sense," Riley said.

"You know I support whatever makes you happy, right?" Olivia asked.

"I know. And I love you for it. But don't worry. It's early days for me and Grey. I can't begin to even think what will happen."

Olivia narrowed her gaze. "I don't want you hurt again, but I do want you to open your heart to possibilities. I did myself and Dylan a true disservice by not doing that."

Nice words, Avery thought, but she'd learned the hard way that by opening her heart up to possibilities, hurt inevitably followed.

When Grey picked up Avery on Thursday evening, the weather was hot and humid, but the sun shone on the horizon, setting in a beautiful explosion of orange, red, and yellow. He'd let nearly a week pass without more than a few texts and little pressure, despite the fact that he craved her with every cell of his being.

Where she'd been a vague dream for the last three months, a goal and hope for the future, since he'd seen her again—spent time with her, *kissed* her—she was now so much more. He wanted a future, and not knowing if she'd come around ate at him more than he wanted to admit. Grey didn't do nervous. Not before a show, not ever.

Yet as they drove over the bridge to Star Island, his stomach was in knots, and he knew why. This was his shot. Avery would meet his friends, see what his life beyond the stage was really like, and she'd judge whether or how she fit in. He had no doubt Lola and Rep would accept her and make her feel at home. But would she relax enough to give them a chance? He felt like a fucking pussy, worrying so damned much.

"Alex used to live here on the island," she said of her half brother, former quarterback for the Tampa Breakers.

Grey was grateful to her for breaking into his thoughts. "It's a great place for people who need privacy." He glanced over at her as he drove.

She nodded. "He liked the area, but I think he was lonely. He and Madison have a smaller house now in a more residential area, and they love it." She adjusted her sunglasses on the bridge of her nose.

He loved how she looked in a strappy, revealing sundress, her hair pulled back in a soft braid. Easy and casual, yet so beautiful she took his breath away.

"So who will be here?" she asked.

"No clue."

She laughed. "That's such a guy answer."

He grinned. "When it comes to Lola, having friends over can mean anything from just me to a houseful of Rep's football buddies. But she did say small."

"Good."

He agreed. The smaller the better. He hadn't seen Lola since their visit with Milo in rehab, and Grey hoped she meant a very few close friends.

"So how was your week?" he asked Avery. He'd missed her, and he wondered if she felt the same.

"Good, except for a hassle with the blog," she said, sounding frustrated.

"What's going on?"

"Trolls. Hackers. I don't know. I keep getting an influx of insulting comments on the daily blog. Same on the videos."

He narrowed his gaze. "Is that normal?"

"Not like this. I've spent hours on the phone with my web people getting them to isolate and shut it down."

A quick look and he caught her massaging her shoulders, her tension obvious. If he weren't driving, he'd love to help her release some of the strain, but he tamped down on his wayward thoughts before they could travel the sexual road and make him any more aware of her in the enclosed car than he already was.

She sighed. "The tech guys explained something about someone spoofing IP addresses and things I don't understand, but they're monitoring things more closely now and removing the comments as they happen."

"What do the comments say?" he asked. Lola and Rep's house came into sight at the end of the long road.

"They're calling me a bitch, a whore, and even . . ." She shook her head and shuddered. "Never mind. Suffice it to say, it's foul."

"What the fuck? Who'd call you names like that?" he asked, pissed off now.

"I don't know. That's why they're called trolls." She placed a hand on his shoulder. "It's common in the blogging world. It's just never happened to me before."

He glanced over and winked, reassuring her he'd relax. But he didn't like the fact that anyone was playing games with her, and he hoped like hell it could be shut down fast.

"It's calmed a little. Hopefully whoever they are, they'll get frustrated with the lack of visibility and go away."

"Let me know if it doesn't stop." He'd call in the best people he could if someone was making her life miserable.

"I can always ask my brothers' IT people to look at things, but when they get involved in my life, things get even messier." She shivered, obviously not thrilled with the idea of bringing in her overprotective brothers who owned Double Down Security.

But her brothers were a solid choice, if it came to that. Even Lola had hired them when she'd moved back to Miami. Grey didn't want a bodyguard trailing him everywhere he went, but the reality was, he never knew if or when he'd be ambushed, so he needed someone he trusted. He didn't think the Dare brothers would want anything to do with protecting his ass, so he'd hired Marco to stay on the job. He wasn't trailing them now, but Grey kept him on the payroll.

He parked at the end of the long drive, with the house right in front of them. Lola and Rep had purchased a white Spanish-style home that suited them.

"The landscaping is gorgeous," Avery murmured, forcing him to see it from her perspective.

Tropical pink flowers, green plants, and palm trees covered the front and allowed for privacy from neighbors who weren't close by anyway.

"It's beautiful."

"So is the house," she murmured. "It's not too modern. And I love the stucco and the adobe-colored roof."

"Me too. But inside? Lola's taste is . . . eclectic. Wait until you see."

He rang the doorbell once and opened the unlocked door, letting them inside as Lola would expect him to. "Hello?" he called out.

"Grey!"

Lola ran toward him, a flash of dark hair and crop top as she jumped into his arms and hugged him tight. "It's been so long!"

A sharp spike of possessiveness ran through Avery, striking her directly in the heart and taking her off guard.

"Lola, let the guy breathe," a deep voice said as a large man with dark hair and plenty of muscles joined them. "Otherwise I'm going to have to hit your best friend, and I know you don't want blood on your freshly painted walls."

Lola jumped down and laughed. "It's so good to see you!"

"Same here," Grey said, immediately reaching for Avery's hand.

The gesture helped calm her nerves and emotions. A little. She really wanted to give the woman a chance, for Grey's sake.

"Lola and Rep, meet Avery Dare. Avery, this is Lola, she's insane, and Rep Grissom."

"It's good to meet you," Rep said, capturing her other hand in his.

She met his blue eyes, struck by how good-looking he was . . . in a bulked-up, beefy-football-player way. "I'm sure we've been in the same room at a Thunder party, but it's good to actually be introduced," she said.

"That's right, you're Ian's little sister."

"It's been a burden," she said, laughing.

Rep glanced at Grey. "I like her."

"I do too." Grey pulled Avery close, wrapping one arm tightly around her. She felt his affection, and more, straight down to her toes.

"I'm so happy you came!" Lola said, still bouncing in excitement, her voice smoky, her Alabama accent obvious. "I've heard so much about you for so many years. I wasn't sure this day would come."

"Give it a rest, Lo," Grey muttered.

Avery melted a little at the knowledge that he'd spoken of her at all. "Thanks for having me over."

"Like I said, it's a pleasure. Now come on in, and let's get to know each other." Lola pulled her away from Grey, and Avery had no choice but to follow the spitfire through her *eclectic* house, passing a huge set of painted lips on a long hallway wall.

Avery had a feeling she was in for an interesting evening.

Chapter Four

Despite Avery's brief flare of jealousy, she liked Lola. Her bubbly personality and genuine warmth were contagious, and it was obvious she only had eyes for Rep and a sisterly affection for Grey. And true to his prediction, they were the only other couple there.

As Lola explained while the men were outside grilling, "I really don't have a lot of friends in Miami, but Rep is based here. I've met a lot of the football wives and significant others, and I like them, but I'm still looking for my own crowd, if you know what I mean."

"I totally do. I have my sister and sisters-in-law, whom I'm close with, and my best friend, Ella, but I like doing my own thing. Next time we all get together, you should join us."

"I'd love to!"

And just like that, a huge rock star was going to hang with Avery and her family. Life had really weird twists and turns.

"Come. Let's get comfortable." Lola gestured toward the oversized sofas. "I've read your blog and watched your videos and I have to say I'm impressed."

Avery was thrilled that someone of Lola Corbin's stature would be interested and find her work good. "Thank you. That means a lot coming from you."

Lola waved away the comment. "I've used many of your suggestions, and they're great. Seriously."

"Well, I bet I can learn a lot from you too." After all, the woman was often onstage, photographed for magazines, and lived a life in the spotlight, so she always had to worry about her appearance.

"We can trade knowledge," Lola said with an easy grin.

"I'll take you up on that." Avery glanced around the large room. A baby grand piano sat in one corner, the sofa was a gorgeous cocoa color, and behind her was yet another mural, this one an abstract of colors washed across the entire wall.

"Your taste is so eclectic," Avery said.

Lola laughed. "That's Grey's word. I'm sure you mean it's all over the place and what the hell were you thinking when you decorated the joint!"

Avery shook her head. "No . . . well, maybe. A little."

"I can't help it. I like what I like. So it's a good thing Rep doesn't care about things like decor."

Avery leaned back against the comfortable cushions. "He cares about you, so the rest doesn't matter."

Lola curled one leg beneath her. "Is that how you are? If you're in love, nothing else matters?" Her blue eyes pinned Avery in place, and the question had Avery choking on her drink. "Sorry. I tend to speak my mind," Lola said, mirth in her gaze and not a hint of true remorse in her voice.

"Yes, I can see that. I take it you're asking about my feelings for Grey?" Avery decided to confront the innuendo head on.

Lola shrugged. "He's my family, and I want him to be as happy as I am. And I know no matter how many years have passed, you've always been important to him. I just want to make sure you're not going to hurt him in the end." Her tone was light, but the warning in her message was clear.

"Wow. You really don't hold back." Avery rubbed her bare arms, chilled by Lola's sudden protectiveness.

Despite the fact that Lola was Grey's best friend, Avery had let her guard down and relaxed around her. She'd invited her out with her closest friends, only to find herself cornered and pushed.

"Look," Avery said, wanting to be perfectly clear. "If anyone's in danger of getting hurt, it's me, so don't worry about your best friend." She heard the sharpness in her voice, but she couldn't bring herself to take it back.

Lola let out a long breath. "I like you, Avery, I really do," she said, her tone softening. "I'm just looking out for Grey. He's been like a brother to me, and it's what I always do."

"Well, Grey can look out for himself. What's going on?" Grey himself asked, stepping into the room, his gaze darting from Lola to Avery.

Avery glanced at Lola and managed a smile. "Not a thing. Just girl talk." She placed her glass on a coaster and rose to her feet. "I'm going to the ladies' room. I'll be right back."

She needed a few minutes to compose herself before she had to face Lola and Grey and the subject of their relationship, because if she knew Grey, he wouldn't buy her story or let things go until he had answers.

Grey watched Avery leave the room before turning on his best friend. "What the fuck did you say to her?" he asked as Rep walked into the room.

"Don't talk to her like that, man." The large football player strode up to his woman and wrapped an arm around her. He leaned down and asked, "Tell me, baby, what'd you do?"

Grey bit the inside of his cheek. Rep might look out for Lola, but he knew her well too.

"It's like Avery said, it was girl talk." Lola blushed but held firm.

Grey cocked an eyebrow her way.

"Fine. It was about you." She pursed her lips, then forced out the rest. "And I might have warned her not to hurt you."

"Dammit, Lo, I wanted her to meet my friends, not face an inquisition."

"You're the one who told me she's wary of the craziness that comes with celebrity. I'm just worried she's going to freak out and bail on you and—"

He stiffened. "It's my problem. Not yours."

"He's right," Rep told her.

Grey groaned. "I'm going to do damage control, and when we come back out, you're going to be your nice, nonprying, nonthreatening self."

"Okay. If it means anything, she seems great," Lola said.

"Then behave. You aren't helping me by driving her away from my best friends." Without waiting for a reply, Grey turned and headed to find Avery.

He approached her as she was coming out of the bathroom and eased her back in the small area, shutting the door behind them. He realized his mistake immediately when his body responded to her nearness and her distinctly warm vanilla scent. Once again, he warned his cock to calm down. Now wasn't the time.

"You okay?" he asked her, taking in her wary expression.

"Why wouldn't I be?"

He narrowed his gaze. "I know Lola said something she shouldn't have."

"It's fine." She flicked her braid over her shoulder dismissively. "We can work it out between the two of us."

He appreciated her attempt to let things go, but he wasn't accepting her easy out. "Not when I'm the issue."

Avery sighed. "Lola is looking out for you, and I respect that even if I don't like her getting involved or questioning my feelings and motives."

"Which she had no right to do. I don't need her fighting my battles or making trouble between us out of some misguided sense of loyalty."

"Don't worry. I'm not going to do something stupid like ask you to choose between me and your best friend."

"There'd be no contest who'd win."

"Good to know." She clenched her jaw, steeled herself, and tried to push past him and get to the door.

Ridiculous woman, he thought, holding her in place with his hips, pressing her against the vanity behind her.

She sucked in a shallow breath, her flushed cheeks revealing she was as hot for him as he was for her. "You need me to explain that better for you, sugar?"

Avery scowled, and that expression set him off. He'd played by her rules, been nice, accommodating, and taken his time. If she didn't believe where she fit in his life, he'd damn well have to show her, he thought and slammed his lips down on hers.

She stiffened at first, her hands coming to his shoulders in a halfhearted attempt to push him away until suddenly things changed. She softened beneath him and kissed him back with the same need driving him, her fingers curling into the material of his shirt. Her teeth clashed with his; their tongues tangled. He slid his hands beneath her dress and cupped her breast through flimsy lace, pinching her nipple between his fingers until she whimpered and bucked against him.

He released the tight bud only to give the other one the same treatment. She pulled at his hair as she cried out, rocking her hips into his, seeking relief against the harsh denim of his jeans. "I need . . . I can't . . ."

"Shh. I'll take care of you," he promised. He lifted her, setting her down on the vanity counter and hiking her dress above her hips.

"Wait, in *here?*" she asked, coming to her senses and drawing her legs together.

"Nobody's going to bother us." He pushed her legs apart and slid her panties down her tanned legs, shoving them into his back pocket.

He looked down at the gorgeous sight. Her bare pussy beckoned, creamy skin and slick folds waiting for him. "Fuck. I've waited years to see this." He cupped her wet heat in his hand, and she gave in.

She leaned against the mirror, head back, cheeks flushed, and a sense of satisfaction flowed through him that she trusted him this way.

"I want to see you come for me, Avery." He slid a finger inside her and nearly came himself at the feel of her tight walls clasping him in heat.

She trembled, and a raw sound ripped from her throat.

"Lean forward." She did as he asked, and he pressed her head against him. "Scream into my shoulder," he said and began pumping his finger in and out, all the while keeping pressure on her clit with his hand.

Her soft sighs and breathy moans let him know what worked, and when he curled his finger upward and her breathing hitched, he knew he'd found *the* spot. He kept up the pressure, rotating his hand in a circular motion until she was writhing on the counter.

He slid his finger out, and her inner walls clasped at him, not wanting to let him go. "Noo . . ."

He grinned and slicked a finger over her clit, focusing on where she needed him the most. Back and forth, he worked the tight bud, and she rotated her hips in time to his rhythm, keeping her on the edge but not taking her over.

"Grey, please, please, please." She was shaking, nearly totally undone and just where he wanted her. Begging him for what he could give her.

Only then did he change the light caress to a hard tweak, and she came, first screaming then fucking biting his shoulder as the remainder of the tremors shook her body.

He held her until her orgasm subsided, ignoring his own pain and state of need.

She lifted her head, her glazed eyes meeting his. "That was . . . earth-shattering."

"I hope so, because it was just the first of many."

Her eyes opened wide. Grey was so on edge he couldn't manage a laugh at her incredulous expression. Her hands drifted to the button on his jeans.

He shook his head and clasped her wrists in his. "If you touch me now, I'll explode."

"That's the idea," she said, treating him to an impish smile.

Hell no, he thought. "The first time I come with you, it's damn well going to be inside that hot pussy."

Those eyes opened even wider at his blunt words.

He adjusted the top of her dress so she looked presentable. He couldn't help it if she still looked almost fucked. Hell, he liked it.

"Where have you been hiding?" she asked, her voice still husky.

"What?"

She bit down on her puffy bottom lip. "You've been so . . ." She wrinkled her nose, searching for the right word. "Gentle up till now." Her soft gaze bored into his, and guilt flooded him.

"Did I go too far? Hurt you?"

"No! I actually like this side of you." A sweet blush stained her cheeks. "I've just never seen it before, and you've definitely kept it from me on purpose."

His heart started beating again at *I actually like this side of you*, and he blew out a long breath.

"You weren't sure about me or us," he said, trying to explain. "It seemed smart to let you set the pace. But when you were about to walk out on me because of Lola . . . I decided to change my game plan."

She studied him in silence for so long he grew antsy, shifting on his feet.

"It's about time," she finally said.

He took that as an all clear. "We're out of here," he muttered.

"Now?" she asked, stunned.

"Yep. I need to be inside you. I'm taking you home before you change your mind."

"But what about Lola? And Rep?"

"Trust me, they'll understand." He grasped her hand and unlocked the door.

"But I'm not wearing my panties."

"So? They're just where I want them," he said, patting his jeans pocket. Without giving her a chance to respond, he pulled her along with him back into the big living room.

"Everything okay?" Lola asked.

"Fine," Avery said.

"Great," Grey added. "I'm sorry to break up the party, but we need to get going." He squeezed Avery's hand in reassurance.

Lola looked from him to Avery, a smile edging her lips as she took them in and understanding dawned. "I can see why," she said, laughing.

Rep chuckled. "Okay then."

"Umm, it was nice to meet you both," Avery said.

Grey headed for the door, tugging her beside him, but she dug in her heels, turning back to the other couple. "Thank you for including me."

Grey understood he needed to let this moment between Avery and Lola happen, and he stopped his run for the exit.

"It was good to meet you," Lola said, her expression as serious as he'd ever seen it. "Come back anytime."

"Thanks," Avery said.

"I mean it!" she called out as Grey started for the front entry once more.

He opened the door and came to a stop when he ran right into his manager about to ring the bell. "Simon." Grey was surprised to find him there.

"Kingston," Simon said by way of greeting.

His gaze zeroed in on Avery, and Grey had the sudden urge to pull her behind him and shield her from his manager, which was ridiculous.

"Lola's inside, but we were just leaving," Grey informed the man.

"Aren't you going to introduce us?" Simon asked, curiosity in his tone.

"Avery Dare," she said herself, extending her hand.

"Simon Colson, and it's a pleasure to meet you. I trust you enjoyed the concert I left you tickets for?"

That night was the last thing Grey wanted in Avery's head now, when he finally had her on the way to his bed.

"I did. The band was amazing," she said, genuine enthusiasm in her voice, and a bit of pride filled him at the knowledge that she had enjoyed the concert.

Simon nodded. "I know it's hectic backstage afterward, but I hope you were able to make good use of the passes?" he asked in a too-kind voice.

Grey swore. The SOB knew full well what had happened that night, and he was deliberately rubbing Avery's face in it. The question was, why? And the only answer he could come up with was that Avery's presence in his life somehow threatened Simon. Which again made no sense, since the man had no idea Grey wasn't keen on using him in any future endeavors.

He tightened his grip on Avery's hand and turned his attention to what was important—Avery, who eyed Simon with a healthy dose of wariness.

"I did get backstage, actually. And you're right. It's a crazy scene," Avery said.

He was surprised she managed to keep her voice and expression neutral.

"Comes with the territory. Especially around our boy here. The women love him." Simon smiled at her.

Grey had had enough, but before he could speak, Avery did.

"They do because he's that talented." She straightened her shoulders and met Simon's gaze. "But as you can see, Grey and I reconnected, and that's all that matters."

Grey grinned. Apparently his girl had solid intuition and knew how to hold her own. She'd managed with Lola and again now with Simon. He hoped she realized her own inner strength.

She turned to Grey, dismissing Simon. "You ready to go home?"

"With you? I was born ready." He glanced at his manager. "I'd say it's nice to see you, but given you're still playing mind games, not so much." He led Avery around Simon and walked out the door.

They settled into his car, and he turned to face her. "We still good?" he asked, hoping that her replies hadn't been a performance for Simon's sake. He didn't want her to return to being worried about the rocker lifestyle.

"Your manager's an ass, but we're fine." She buckled her seat belt and met his gaze.

"We don't need to talk?"

"Is that what you really want to do now?" She snaked a hand across the seat and settled her warm palm on his thigh. "Because I thought we had bigger, more important plans." Her hand slid upward, closer to his aching cock.

Message received, Grey thought, turning on the ignition and heading out.

Avery's thoughts were running all over the place. If she put aside the fact that her underwear was in Grey's pocket, the most prevalent thought in her head was taking back control. She wasn't going to let her fears stop her from experiencing what was bound to be the best sex of her life with a man she still had deep feelings for. Nor would she allow Grey's manager to run her off. And for whatever reason, that had been his intent. His polite British accent hadn't covered the fact that he'd intentionally tried to intimidate and scare her by reminding her of all the women who surrounded and wanted Grey.

For right now, Grey was here with her. But she'd seen him signing autographs and on the stage, and there, he was in his element. She wouldn't want to take that sense of self away from him and knew better than to believe that he suddenly desired a normal life away from the fans and the spotlight. But she did think he believed it, when in reality, all he needed was a break from the insanity of being on the road.

At some point, boredom and the need for more would reassert themselves; but as long as she was aware that day was coming, she could keep this *thing* between them in perspective. She was an adult, perfectly capable of handling a short-term relationship. She wouldn't insult Grey or what they shared by calling it an affair. When it came to them together, it was always so much more. It just couldn't be forever.

She swallowed hard, locking the harsh truth away in a box where it couldn't hurt her. Just like she'd boxed away her father's choices, which had never included her. Unless he'd needed her . . . nope. That wasn't pushing things away.

"You're quiet," Grey said, intruding on her not-so-pleasant thoughts.

"Just thinking," she said.

"About?"

"Us." She shook her head, clearing it of all negative emotions. "Can't you drive faster?" She didn't want anything to intrude on what they had planned, and this trip without panties was making her antsy and needy. Even now, without underwear, she was wet.

His laughter rumbled through her and set her on fire, bringing her back to the moment in the bathroom. She'd never come so hard, so fast. In the years since Grey, she'd chosen men who were the opposite of her ex. Safe men. Men who didn't challenge her, who didn't excite her . . . who didn't remind her of Grey.

Now was the time to live in the moment. Avery had never been good at doing that, but dammit, she was going to try.

They pulled up to a luxury condo complex, a high-rise building with a security guard in the lobby. Grey kept a hand on her back and led her into the elevator that, with his personal key card, took them directly to his floor.

Her body tingling with anticipation, they stepped into his apartment, and he shut the door and locked it behind them. The sound reverberated through her with finality, putting punctuation on what they had planned.

"Grey, I—" She never finished her sentence. No sooner had the lock clicked than she found herself against the wall, Grey's lips on hers.

She didn't hesitate to wrap her arms around his neck and kiss him back for all she was worth.

Today had taught her something. It was one thing for her to back away from Grey out of fear, another for someone to try to take him from her. Two someones in the span of half an hour. At least that's what Lola's warning and Simon's boasting about women loving Grey had felt like. She needed to take control of the situation and do what she wanted. She needed to stop letting even her own insecurities and fear get the better of her. She was here, and she was with Grey.

He was relentless, his lips devouring hers, and while last time she'd been the one taking, this time she wanted to give. She wanted to feel, taste, and experience him in living, breathing color. She pulled up his shirt, and he yanked it off, giving her an entire blank slate to enjoy. She ran her hands over his taut abs, his hard stomach, and smooth, tanned, tattoo-covered skin. Every touch aroused her senses, and she leaned in close, inhaling, drinking in his familiar musk-laden scent.

Unable to resist temptation, she licked his chest, eliciting a shuddering moan from him. She grinned. "You like that."

"And you like that I do." He grasped her wrists, pinning them against the wall.

She sucked in a breath and met his darkened gaze.

"Grey?" she asked, surprised by both his sudden show of dominance and how much she enjoyed it.

Her sex was slick with arousal, and she rolled her hips into him, his thick cock nestling in the cradle of her thighs, fire burning her inside and out.

"I promised myself the first time I'd take things slow, but when you touch me, I'm afraid I'll go off and ruin everything. So I need you to promise to keep your hands here." He still held her wrists against the wall.

"Since when are there restrictions between us?" Feeling daring, she licked him again, this time running her tongue over his nipple.

His body shook at her touch. "Since when don't you play fair?" he asked, lifting her into his arms.

She squealed and wrapped her legs around his hips, her sandals falling to the floor.

He walked her into his unlit bedroom and settled her in the center of a king-size bed.

He flicked on a small bedside lamp. "Be right back," he said and strode to the bathroom.

Avery's pulse pounded, and need thundered through her veins. In keeping with her new promise to take what she wanted, she reached for the hem of her dress and drew it over her head just as he strode back toward her, condoms in hand.

He stopped short, treating her to a low whistle. "Memories didn't do you justice, sugar."

She was more modest than not and did her best not to squirm as his hot gaze raked over her. Not knowing what turn the night would take, she'd chosen her favorite bra and panty set, a mix of white silk and lace. Of course the underwear was long gone, and judging by his reaction, he was extremely pleased with what he saw.

"Now how about you let me test my memories some more?" she asked.

His cut upper body already had her primed and ready. She couldn't imagine what the sight of that hidden but impressive bulge behind the denim would do to her.

"Whatever you want," he said and tossed the condoms onto the bed. His hands went to the button on his jeans, stripping himself out of them in record time.

And then it was her turn to swallow a groan and stare. Either her memories were wrong or time had filled him out everywhere. His thick erection held her attention, and she ran her tongue over her lips, contemplating what she wanted to do to him first.

She reached out and wrapped her hand over the steely velvet shaft, gliding up and down, testing her limits.

"Harder," he said through clenched teeth.

She swallowed hard and followed instructions, pumping his erection up and down until slick precum covered the plump head.

"Enough."

She was smart enough to recognize he'd given her all he could, at least for the moment, and she released him, missing his hard, hot heat immediately.

He unhooked her bra in a deft move she didn't want to consider too closely. After sliding the garment down her arms and tossing it aside, he tackled her onto the bed, her naked body colliding with his. Heat and hardness seeped into her pores, and she took a moment, a deep breath, to savor the feeling of Grey after so many years.

He was more muscular, firmer, more solid than she remembered but every inch the man she'd missed.

"I can't believe it's you," he said gruffly, his words eerily mimicking her thoughts.

She smiled even though he couldn't see. "I know the feeling," she murmured, running her hands along the rippling muscles of his back.

He braced his arms on either side of her and pushed himself up. She met his gaze, trying her best not to lose herself in the green depths. He kissed her then, more gently than the rushed fervor of before, as if them being skin to skin at last had eased something inside him. She knew it felt that way for her.

He grasped her hands, pulling them above her head, while his lower body rocked against hers, his thick shaft rubbing against her clit, the motion causing a rising tide of desire to sweep through her. His firm cock slicked over her damp sex, insistently taking her higher yet leaving her achingly empty inside.

She moaned and lifted her knees, bringing him in fuller contact. She needed more. So much more. But he was in no rush, and his next words confirmed it.

"There are so many things I want to do before I come inside you."

"Like what?" she asked, her body shaking with unfulfilled need.

"First I want to taste you here." He leaned down and pulled her nipple into his mouth, swirling his tongue over the tip.

Already sensitive from his earlier play at Lola's, she sucked in a breath and attempted to ease herself away. He immediately soothed her with loving laps of his tongue, both on the tight bud and the tender area surrounding it. He took his time, kissing her, nuzzling with his nose and lips before licking at her once more. Her sex clenched, and she felt his ministrations deep in her core.

"I need you," she said, arching into him, wanting more of those sweet licks. They felt so good that she was actually building toward climax from his tongue on her breasts and nipples when suddenly he released one with a pop, leaving her bereft.

"Grey," she whimpered, and attempted to ease her hand down to cup his erection. Anything to move things along.

"Uh-uh, sugar. Hands back over your head. I'm not finished yet."

"But I need to touch you."

"And I need to taste you some more first."

She gave in, but she was going to make him pay for this slow, sensual torture. He slid down her body, his lips trailing over her ribs and abdomen until his face was mere inches from her sex, his warm breath fanning her clit. Fireworks flashed in front of her eyes, bright in color and size. And that was before he parted her outer lips with his thumbs and ran his tongue along her slick flesh, once, twice, pulling each one into his mouth before releasing it and licking her once more.

He glanced up, meeting her gaze with a wicked one of his own. "You taste like sugar," he murmured, and she knew she'd never think of that endearment the same way again.

Her hips bucked, and he read her signals correctly because he put his talented mouth to even better use. He licked, ate, nibbled, and teased her pussy, pushing her past restraint, into ever-sharper awareness. Considering she'd been primed for what felt like hours, she was so damned close already.

She thrust her pelvis up, grinding into his mouth, needing the pressure of his lips, the suckling, and the occasional gentle scrape of his teeth. She shattered, taking her pleasure, her orgasm coming in waves that seemed to never end. She clenched and unclenched her fists above her head, bound by his words and her unspoken promise. Unable to touch him or ground herself, she rode out her climax, grasping at air with her fingers. He didn't let up until the tremors subsided, and she fell limp against the mattress, her arms still useless over her head.

The sound of ripping foil reawakened her senses, and she opened her eyes to find Grey poised over her, the hard tip of his erection nudging her sex.

"You're gorgeous when you come, sugar," he said, eyes glittering, jaw hard and taut.

She bit down on her lower lip, embarrassed . . . and yet . . . not. Because it was Grey.

"It's my turn to see you come apart," she said, arching her hips and attempting to pull his cock into her needy core.

But he held out. He was barely inside her, a mere tease of what could be, and he still clearly maintained control. Unacceptable, she thought. She wanted to render him senseless. She needed to see it, to believe she had the same power over him that he clearly had over her.

Finished following his rules, she ran her hands down his chest, scoring his skin lightly with her nails, scraping over his dark nipples. He groaned and arched his hips, causing him to slide deeper.

"Fuck it," he muttered and thrust his hips, filling her completely.

"Grey." She sucked in a startled breath, unprepared for the flood of emotion that rushed her from all sides. A harsh combination of panic and fear that the feelings surrounding her were too close to love.

"I feel it too," he said, as if he understood she needed the reassurance.

But he couldn't know. Couldn't possibly still possess the emotions threatening to pull her under and prevent her from walking away from this, from him, unscathed.

She blinked back the tears that threatened, and when he shifted and began to move, nothing else mattered. His solid thrusts took her out of herself until she was aware of only Grey and the pounding of his body against and into hers as he took her into an explosive orgasm that consumed her, body and soul.

Chapter Five

Night crept into morning. Grey woke Avery up once by settling between her thighs and licking her sweet pussy until she began yanking his hair and coming hard, only then realizing it wasn't a dream, and a second time by pulling her back against him and fucking her from behind. They fit like two pieces of a puzzle. She filled the holes he'd always been aware of and some he hadn't known existed. He still had shit from his past to fix. Avery gave him hope that he could do that soon. She gave him hope, period, and Grey wasn't letting her go.

A cute snore sounded from the other side of the bed. He debated waking her up again but decided against it, instead heading for the kitchen to fill another kind of hunger. He was drinking a cup of coffee when he heard a sound.

He turned to see her walk into the kitchen, wearing nothing but one of his T-shirts. Long legs she'd had wrapped around him last night beckoned to him. Her hair fell in messy waves, the blonde streaks appearing like a halo around her makeup-free yet still beautiful face.

He wanted to drag her back to bed but offered her food instead. "Coffee? Muffin?"

Her eyes opened wide at the last choice. "Muffin, please. I'm starving."

He chose not to touch that remark or she'd never get her food. "I'll run downstairs and grab us some from the corner bakery."

Violet eyes met his. "How about we pick them up together? I have to go home soon, shower and change. I have a meeting at the hospital."

He pushed aside the disappointment that she was leaving so soon. "Today?"

She shrugged. "That's when the head of the Children's Committee can meet. I have an idea I need him to approve."

He drank the last of his caffeine fix and put the mug in the sink. "What's your idea?"

She blushed but explained, "Ella and I want to throw a prom for the teenagers in treatment."

He blinked, surprised. "What do you mean?"

"I don't think these kids have enough to look forward to. There's a lot they miss out on. I saw the idea on the news. Memorial Sloan Kettering Children's Hospital in New York ran the event last year. I have the connections to make it happen here. I want to bring in a makeup team, a hair team, wigs for those cancer patients who have lost their hair." Her hands flew with expressiveness as she continued. "With Ella's help, because she works with designers, I can get dresses donated, and these kids can go to their own prom. Imagine how excited they'd be!"

Her enthusiasm sparkled in her eyes, determination in her voice and expression. He loved watching her get so animated about a subject.

He leaned back against the kitchen counter, the cold granite at his back. "I don't think anyone will be able to resist your enthusiasm," he said, awed by both the idea and the selflessness behind it. When she'd given bone marrow at such a young age, the choice hadn't been hers exactly, but now the way she gave back, it was.

"I hope you're right. Dr. McCann holds tight to those purse strings, but I already have promises of people and businesses who will donate, so I'm sure that will help the cause." She blew out a long breath and laughed. "Jeez, enough about me. What are you doing today?"

He ran a hand through his hair. "Not sure. I was thinking about visiting my mom but . . ." He trailed off, wishing he'd never brought up the idea.

"But what?" she asked.

He turned away, not wanting to admit how badly he'd screwed up with his family. Avery had issues with her father, but her old man deserved it. Grey's mother was selfless and wonderful, and he hadn't understood her. Hadn't treated her with the love and respect she deserved. If he told Avery, she'd be disappointed in him, and he wasn't sure he could handle seeing condemnation in her eyes when he admitted that he hadn't been home to visit since his return to Miami.

"Grey?" Avery placed a hand on his arm, bringing him back to the present.

"I haven't been over to see her yet."

"What? Why not?"

He blew out a deep breath and turned to face her, finding Avery looking concerned as she stared at him. "I just haven't been back in a while."

"What's *a while?*" she astutely asked.

He closed his eyes as he answered. "Years."

He let the word hang in the air while she digested the information. Even to Grey, it was ironic. When he was struggling and later making some money, he'd come home. Called often. Once he'd hit the big time, he hadn't had time to visit. Hadn't made time, he amended. Oh, he'd sent money, bought his mother and stepdad a house, provided items that he thought they should have to make their lives easier.

None of which made them happy. Having each other made them happy. A visit from Grey would make his mother ecstatic. And he hadn't given her that. Because he was ashamed.

"Grey, *why?* You love your mom, and I know she loves you."

"I . . ." He stammered, searching for the right words to explain the inexplicable. "For years I was embarrassed about my stepfather's job as a janitor. Even though it was perfectly respectable and honest work, work that put food on the table." He shook his head, remembering how he'd avoid the hallways if he saw his stepdad at school, ducking the other way.

"You never said anything to me."

"Because I was humiliated. Your father owned buildings; my parents cleaned them." He hated how shallow it all sounded now. "That judgment I felt, it was part of my need to run, to get away and make something of myself."

"I thought that had to do with how your real father treated you," she said quietly.

"It was, in part." Grey's biological father had molded his mind and warped his perspective in so many ways. "I wanted to be better than the good-for-nothing son he said I was. Although my brain didn't work like his or my sister, Julia's, *I* was worth something," he said, jabbing himself in the chest.

He felt a pinch and looked down to see Avery's nails curling into his arm. "You're worth everything," she whispered.

He shook his head, unable to let himself believe her words. Maybe one day, when he'd made things right at home, he'd appreciate what she was saying. "I didn't treat my mom or Ricardo any better than my father treated me. I didn't realize it until . . ."

"Go on. Say it. Whatever it is, get it out." At some point, she'd come up beside him, her soft body curled into his, as if she knew he needed her close.

He blew out a breath, dizzy with the words bouncing around his brain. "I never understood her second marriage or their happiness at just being together until I had everything . . . and realized I was still empty inside." That was the point when he'd decided he needed to walk away from that life and come back, find the person he used to be. Find Avery.

"Oh, Grey."

He shook his head hard. "Don't feel sorry for me. I don't deserve it. I'm more ashamed of how I felt about them than I ever was *of* them."

She stepped in front of him and clasped his face in her hands. "That's why you're such a good man. You aren't your father. You learn from your mistakes. So you were young and stupid." She shrugged. "Your mother loves you. Not only will she understand, she'll be so happy to see you she won't even think about the past."

But he would. He'd remember the real estate listings he'd sent them for mansions that required servants, not understanding when they'd turned him down. He wanted them to have anything he could afford. He hadn't begun to comprehend at the time that money couldn't buy happiness or fulfillment. Now he knew differently.

Now he had to face them again. And he didn't want to do it alone. "I know I shouldn't ask, but will you go with me to visit them? After your meeting."

"Of course I will," she said, her eyes suspiciously damp.

"Thank you."

She smiled. "Now can we get dressed so I can eat my muffin?"

He was ready for a mood lightener. "Not unless I can eat your muffin first." He squeezed her ass in his hand.

She squealed and turned, taking off for the bedroom. He followed . . . and it was a long while before they made it downstairs to the bakery.

He drove her home, and she kissed him good-bye and ran into her building, last night's clothes balled in her hand, his T-shirt and a pair of old running shorts on her sexy body.

Avery made it home from Grey's, waved to Ella, and rushed to shower and get ready for their appointment at the hospital. She was running late, which left no time for conversation about Avery's love life on the way to the hospital. Instead they prepped for the meeting.

By the time they had survived the pitch and discussion with the ever-so-pleasant Dr. McCann, Avery was exhausted. And being woken up by Grey's tongue and other body parts last night was only part of the reason. She was sore in places she hadn't known existed, and muscles she'd rarely used felt a sweet ache that reminded her of Grey. She'd done her best to keep her mind on task and any goofy smile off her face during the meeting. She'd have plenty of time to revisit things later and sort out her overwhelming feelings.

By the time she walked out of their meeting with Dr. McCann, she was glad she'd scheduled the meeting before Ella's upcoming business trip, so she could have her friend there with her, pushing the cause. Ella often volunteered too, both of them having a unique perspective and understanding of both the patients and their situations. The prom was a dream they shared, and both were determined to make something special happen for these children.

Dr. McCann had been his usual dour self, but he was impressed with the idea. Avery waited until they rounded a corner, made certain they were alone, and turned to her friend.

"Well? What's your take?"

Ella leaned against the nearest wall and groaned. "I'm cautiously optimistic. I just got the feeling that he didn't think we could pull this off with no budget. Easier to put the load on us than to just say no," she muttered.

Avery nodded. "That's his MO. But we are going to show him what happens when he challenges two determined women. At least he said we can hold the event at the hospital. I'd have been willing to ask my father for a ballroom at his hotel, but then the most critically ill kids would have missed out." And those were the kids whose smiles she wanted to see the most. "And this way, nobody has to leave the premises. They'll have medical staff and equipment surrounding them should they need it."

Ella's eyes swam with relief at that too. "So venue is one thing we can cross off our to-do list." She glanced at her notepad. Avery had a similar list in her purse. "But now we have to find music, get the food donated, handle setup and clean up ourselves, not to mention everything we already have to plan for preprom."

Avery nodded. "Dresses for the girls, tuxedoes for the boys, the makeup, hair . . ." Her shoulders drooped as the list grew. "And Dr. McCann won't agree until we have all our i's dotted and t's crossed."

"In blood," Ella muttered.

Avery blew out a long breath meant to be agreement. "But we can do this." It would take every bit of persistence and all of the connections they had, but Avery had faith.

"We can," Ella agreed. "So now that that's settled, tell me about last night. Because I can't remember the last time you didn't come home. Or remember to text or call if you weren't." She folded her arms over her chest and pinned Avery with her best mom stare.

Avery winced. "I'm sorry if you were worried."

"I knew you were with Grey, so I wasn't worried. I am, however, curious."

"It was . . . amazing," Avery admitted, feeling her cheeks blush and her body flush with warmth.

"I'm really happy for you. I knew you two had unresolved feelings," Ella said, sounding pleased with her powers of deduction.

"Yes, well, we're working out those feelings."

"In bed." Ella grinned.

Avery rolled her eyes. "Whatever. I'm just taking it one day at a time."

"And that's an improvement over the way you felt last time we spoke." Ella glanced at her phone, reminding Avery she hadn't checked hers since before the meeting.

She pulled her cell from her purse and realized she had six missed calls, some duplicates from various siblings. "So many missed calls," she said, concerned something was wrong.

"Is everything okay?" Ella asked.

"I'm not sure. Maybe one of them left a text." If not, she'd be calling them ASAP.

She opened her text messages, and Olivia's name popped up first. She read out loud. "*Click this link, then call me.*"

Avery clicked on a link to today's local newspaper. And a photo of her and Grey leaving his apartment this morning showed up on her screen. She wore his too-long T-shirt and a pair of gym shorts, her dress and shoes from last night in her hands. And the headline screamed out at her in all capital letters . . . *REASON FOR TANGLED ROYAL BREAKUP!*

"Oh my God," she said as the blood rushed from her head.

"Whoa." Ella led her to a set of chairs down the hall and eased her into the first seat. "Breathe," she instructed.

Avery pulled in deep breaths, trying to calm down and not end up having a panic attack.

"Let me see that." Ella took Avery's phone and stared at the screen. "Well, shit."

"No wonder everyone's been calling me." Her siblings would see this article and know she'd immediately stress.

She was going to have to reassure them she was okay, even if her heart was racing, her hands were shaking, and she still had flashing spots in front of her eyes.

"This is from this morning. I didn't even see anyone watching us." Where had they been? How had she not known her photo had been taken? "How did they know to wait outside his building?" she asked Ella.

"I'm sure that's standard operating procedure for the paparazzi," her friend said, her hand still on Avery's back.

How did Grey live like this? she wondered.

"How are you holding up?" Ella asked, concerned.

Avery swallowed hard. "Not well. I'm going to be a public pariah. The woman who broke up America's favorite band." She shivered at the very idea of that kind of awful publicity.

The fact that it was all lies didn't matter. People believed what they read, she thought. And worse, the drama probably wasn't over. This kind of publicity was part of Grey's life. If their relationship continued, she'd be continually sucked into the drama and made the focus of media scrutiny, she thought, a sudden headache building behind her eyes.

"Hey. One problem at a time, right? Let's get through this situation before we worry about what happens next. Come on. Let's get you home."

"Good idea." She had a sudden yearning for the quiet of her apartment, where she could relax and think things through. Avery rose to her feet and Ella followed. "I'll be fine," she said out loud, trying to convince herself. And she was, until she arrived at her apartment complex to find reporters waiting outside her building.

"Holy shit," Ella muttered. "We're going to make a run for it, okay?"

Stunned, Avery nodded.

They shouted questions at her as she and Ella rushed toward the entrance.

"Avery, how's it feel to break up one of the biggest bands in the country?"

"Avery, any regrets about taking Grey away from the band and dragging him to Miami?"

"Avery, anything to say to the disappointed fans?"

Past memories mixed with the present. The men with cameras closed in on her as she made her way to the entrance. Ella grabbed the handle and pushed Avery inside, slamming the door shut behind her.

Avery breathed out a harsh breath.

"Assholes," Ella muttered.

"Let's get upstairs."

Ella grabbed her hand, and they ran for the elevator.

A few minutes later, Avery was safely inside her apartment. Her heart pounded and sweat dripped off her body. She ducked into the bathroom and splashed cold water on her face and cooled herself off. Calming down didn't happen as easily, and she barely refrained from throwing up.

She didn't know how to process what had just happened. Her worst nightmares about Grey had come to pass, and she didn't know how to handle it.

After taking Avery home, Grey worked out in the gym of his building, opting for a hardcore treadmill run instead of going outside and dealing with fans stopping him along the way. Sweating and tired, he walked back into his apartment and picked up his cell to check messages. He wondered if Avery's meeting had been successful, but he hadn't heard from her. But he did have a shit ton of alerts.

He glanced at Lola's text first. *Read and call me ASAP.* He clicked the accompanying link, took one look at the photo from the local morning paper of Avery and him, and his blood pressure soared through the roof.

"Fuck!" He barely stopped himself from throwing his phone into the nearest wall. Just when things were falling into place with Avery, this happened. Publicity she didn't want with a negative spin guaranteed to cause her trouble and pain.

His blood boiling, he scrolled through the rest of his texts, including one from Simon with a thumbs-up, way-to-go message. *All publicity is good publicity.*

"Asshole," Grey muttered. The man made money off them any way he could and knew that any media attention sold music.

Grey looked at his e-mail next, scrolling through until something that looked like fan mail stopped him cold. His e-mail went through Simon's agency. Always. Grey's personal address was off-limits, and he went to great lengths to keep it that way.

Chills traveled through him as he read:

Dear Lover,

You betrayed me. You know we are meant to be together, but you are fucking that whore. I saw her leave your apartment this morning. That should be me. It will be me. I tried to be nice, to send her messages on her blog, but she isn't getting the hint to leave you alone. Don't worry. I will take care of things so we can finally be together.

Love, now and forever,

Emerald

Emerald. Emerald. He racked his brain for a connection, and suddenly he remembered one. At the fan event Simon had arranged before their last few concerts in Miami, Grey had been in a particularly good mood, since their touring days were coming to an end. He'd had his game face on, flirting with female fans, keeping them happy and engaged.

A woman had approached him wearing a sparkling green shirt, extremely low cut, her red hair sprayed hard. She'd leaned over the table, getting too close as she'd asked for an autograph. Marco had stepped forward, and Grey had known he had to get the woman out of there fast.

He'd winked at her and asked, "What's your name, or should I just call you Emerald, to match your shirt . . . and your eyes." Corny, but she'd eaten it up.

Unfortunately he'd had to sign her chest and not a photo, after which she'd deliberately flashed not just her tit but also her nipple before Marco had grabbed her elbow and escorted her to the next guard at the exit. It wasn't a sight Grey wanted to remember, and he'd put it and her out of his mind almost immediately. But clearly *she* recalled the meeting much differently and put much more meaning into it. Now all the crazy in his life was invading Avery's.

Grey swore out loud. Could this fucking day get any worse? It was like the universe was conspiring to keep them apart, placing every potential obstacle in their path. This Emerald chick had been stalking and sabotaging Avery's blog, and to make matters even worse, the media had painted a target on Avery's back by accusing her of breaking up the band. The exact kind of publicity she sought to avoid.

He didn't know if she'd seen the article yet. If not, he wanted to tell her in person. If she had, he needed to get over to her place and exercise some damage control as soon as possible.

While Ella showered and finished packing in preparation for overseeing a two-week photo shoot on a Caribbean island, Avery returned concerned phone calls. When disaster and insanity struck, the Dare family banded together . . . well, all of them except her father. Apparently he only surfaced when he needed Avery's help for his other kids. Checking on her after she became front-page news must not be a priority for him, she thought, pushing the painful reality away. She didn't need him. She had the rest of her clan circling the wagons. Even her half siblings checked in, with Alex threatening to kick Grey's ass—an act she didn't need or want—and Jason and Sienna each offering her a place to hide out if things became too much.

Olivia and her mother had left messages for Avery on her cell and at home. She'd already called them back and promised she was dealing well with the publicity on her end. They didn't have to know she'd already had a mini panic attack and taken her pills, or that crazy photographers were still camped outside her apartment. They'd just worry, and her mother had a wedding to plan, and her sister was pregnant. Neither needed added stress.

She'd called her brothers back too, reaching Ian and Scott but not Tyler. And that scared her because there was a very good chance Tyler would take one look at the article and, when he couldn't immediately reach Avery on her cell, head right over.

A loud knock sounded on the door. "Avery, open up. It's Tyler."

"And right on time," she muttered, letting her brother in.

"Jesus, there's a massive group of paparazzi out there. Is this what being with that asshole is doing to your life?"

Tyler stood in the doorway, looking less than pleased and ready to take over, something she would not let happen. "If you want to talk to me, back off about Grey. That's not going to help matters."

"Who's causing all the racket?" Ella asked.

Avery turned. Ella had joined them wearing a short silk bathrobe, towel drying her hair as she walked. "Tyler!" she stopped short and stared in shock. Her hand slowly lowered, and the towel dropped to the floor.

"Yes," Avery said. "My bossy brother's here to—"

"Check up on you," Tyler said to Avery . . . but his gaze never wavered from Ella, whose cheeks turned a rosy shade of pink.

"You, go put some clothes on," Tyler ordered her.

"Tyler!" Avery called him out for bossing Ella around in her own apartment.

Ella, meanwhile, frowned at him, then bent to retrieve her towel. Her robe gaped open, exposing her breasts, something she didn't realize until a low growl came from Tyler's throat.

Ella rose and glanced down. "Shit." She spun around and stormed out of the room.

"What was *that* all about?" Avery asked her brother. "Are you trying to be an asshole today? Oh, wait, it just comes naturally."

Tyler blew out a frustrated breath. "Don't change the subject. I'm here to talk about you."

Avery shook her head, feeling like she was missing something. Ella knew Tyler, just like she knew the rest of Avery's siblings, from the two weeks every summer and occasional holidays she'd spent visiting. Had this just been embarrassment? Or something more?

"Avery, I'm worried about you," he said, his voice softening. "You have a history of anxiety—"

"And I'm on daily medication." And had Xanax for emergencies like today. "I'm fine." Or she had been until Grey's life had exploded around her. But she didn't want her brother to worry. "I'm not nine years old anymore," she added as a means of reassuring them both.

Tyler ran a hand through his dark hair. "Between the picture in the paper, the nasty insinuation about breaking up the band, and now the photographers stalking your apartment, you're in the center of the storm. And considering I do security for a living, I should know."

Another loud knock sounded on her door.

"Ask who it is."

Avery shot Tyler a disgusted look. Did he really think she didn't know how to take care of herself?

Instead of asking, she looked through the peephole and groaned. "It's Grey," she said to Tyler and winced inwardly.

The very last thing she needed was a confrontation between Grey and her overprotective brother. But it seemed that was exactly what she was about to get.

Chapter Six

rey couldn't believe he had to cut through paparazzi to get into Avery's building. If he'd known, he'd have found out whether there was a back entrance or brought Marco. The assholes yelled rude questions and tried to crowd him, and it took too damn long to make his way inside. His stomach churned as he imagined what Avery was thinking or feeling. She hated the overzealous female fans, and she'd never been one for large groups of people in general. He just wasn't sure how she'd handle this. Nor did it help to know that getting rid of him would be the easiest option.

He knocked on her door, unsure if she was home. She hadn't answered her phone when he'd called on his way over.

The door opened wide. One look at her face and he swore out loud. "I'm sorry," he said before she could utter a word.

"You damn well should be, Kingston."

He glanced over her shoulder to find one of her brothers standing behind her, arms crossed over his chest as he glared at Grey.

Avery, her face already pale and makeup free, groaned and gestured for him to come inside. "You remember my brother Tyler," she said.

Grey inclined his head at the pissed-off man. Tyler, the brother who'd been in the army, who ran the security company, and who rightfully hated Grey's guts. *Good to see you, man*, wasn't going to cut it.

"What do you want?" Tyler asked.

Avery turned to her brother. "I have enough to deal with without you making things worse. If you can't be civil to Grey, you can leave."

Well, at least she wasn't throwing him out yet. "I came as soon as I saw the article. I had no idea the paps had found you."

"Well, now you know," Tyler said. "And you showing up here is only going to make things worse. We're going to have to put a security detail on you," he said to Avery.

She shook her head. "No way. I can't live like that."

Grey remained silent as the siblings went at it. Until he knew where everyone's head was, he wouldn't step in.

"Well, can you live like this?" Tyler swept an arm toward the window. "Going through that crowd by yourself every time you want to come and go?"

"No, I don't want that." Avery clasped her hands around her forearms in a defensive gesture that gutted Grey.

He'd put her in this position. Somehow, he needed to get her out. Though he might agree with Tyler about security, her brother's strong-arm tactics were only hurting her more, taking away the feelings of control she was holding onto.

Grey shot Tyler a warning look and moved in, leading her to the couch in her living room. He sat down beside her, keeping her close. "Listen, your brother's right. We have to talk about security for you, but we can figure out something that will make you comfortable."

"None of this would be necessary if you'd just disappear," Tyler added. "She could stay with one of us for a little while, they'd forget all about her, and that would be that."

Grey stiffened, bristling at her brother's words, which had too much truth in them for his peace of mind.

"Tyler, go home, please? I'll figure out what I want to do and let you know."

His gaze softened as he looked at his sister. "I'm worried about you. Did you have a panic attack getting through those jackals?" he asked.

Grey narrowed his gaze. "Panic attack?"

Avery tensed. "I handled it."

Tyler placed a hand on her shoulder. "I never said you didn't. I just want to protect you from having to deal with it at all."

"Well, you can't protect me from everything."

But Grey wanted to. He had the overwhelming need to pack her up and move her in with him, into his doorman building, where she'd be protected and safe.

"I'll call the cops to clear them off of private property," Tyler said.

Grey nodded. "That'll be a start, but it won't hold off the more determined ones. And it won't keep them away from public areas where Avery goes."

"Hello, can you stop speaking about me as if I'm not right here?"

Grey met her gaze. "Sorry, sugar."

Tyler scowled at the endearment. "You need a bodyguard. Someone who can follow you at a distance but who will be there just in case you need him. I'm assuming Mr. Rock Star here has one."

Grey stiffened but let the insulting tone slide. "When I know I'll be in public, yes, I have security."

"I want my guy on you when you're together."

"Fine," Grey said, knowing better than to argue. He didn't care who watched their backs as long as she was safe.

"Are we in agreement?" Tyler met his sister's gaze.

Avery groaned. "Fine."

Grey didn't like what he had to do next, but he looked at Tyler. "Can I have a word with you?"

Avery's gaze shot between them. "What? Why?"

"It'll be fine." He leaned over and kissed her cheek.

She stood, and he rose with her.

"I'll go see if Ella's okay." She looked between them one more time. "And I expect an explanation later."

Grey waited until she'd disappeared down the hall before turning to Tyler. "Look, you don't have to like me, but can we agree we both have Avery's best interests at heart?"

"That remains to be seen."

Grey swallowed a curse. The man wasn't going to make anything easy. "There's another security issue you need to know about."

"What's going on?" Tyler asked.

"I got a piece of fan mail . . ." Grey went on to explain the connection between the e-mail he'd received from Emerald and Avery's blog, and the woman's implied threat to break them apart.

He wanted nothing more than to hide the information that would give Avery's brothers even more reason to dislike him and want him away from their sister. But he wouldn't put his self-interest above Avery's safety, and he wasn't foolish enough to think he could handle things on his own.

He rolled his shoulders, tension settling there like lead. "I don't know what it means, but I don't like what my gut's telling me."

"Fuck. And you can't just walk away and leave my sister alone?" Tyler muttered.

Grey had had enough. He stepped into Tyler's personal space. "Listen carefully. I may let you get away with the occasional insult because I know I brought this shit into her life."

"Not to mention how badly you hurt her when you left? Who do you think picked up the pieces? The same people who are going to have to do it when you bail on her again."

"I'm not going anywhere," he said through gritted teeth. "I'm serious about your sister, and you'd better get used to it. In the meantime, I'd appreciate it if you'd use your expertise to help keep her safe."

Tyler eyed Grey warily, but Grey thought he caught a hint of admiration in the man's gaze when he didn't back down.

"Fine. I'll do my job and keep an eye on you at the same time," Tyler said.

"I wouldn't expect anything less. Now, you mentioned anxiety."

Tyler straightened his shoulders. "Not my story to tell."

Grey inclined his head. He wanted to hear anything about Avery from Avery. "Can you at least tell me if I should let her know about the crazy fan?"

Tyler blew out a harsh breath. "I'm torn between honesty and whether or not this will put her over the edge." He paused in thought. "Tell you what. Send me the e-mail, and I'll shoot you one back with the information I need in order to dig into who sent it. Let me get to work on the e-mail and look into her blog. If I find out we're dealing with someone seriously unhinged, I'll let you know, and we'll change tactics."

Grey nodded. He was clearly in the dark about Avery in ways he hadn't expected. He needed to trust her brother's judgment.

"I hate lying, even by omission," he said, his voice low. "But I don't want to freak her out either."

Tyler ran a hand through his hair, which was slightly longer than a military cut. "I know. I don't want her blindsided, but I also don't want her under a crazy amount of stress. Not until we see how badly this current band-breakup news is going to get for her. So we're agreed?"

He nodded. "Agreed." He extended a hand, a peace offering of sorts toward Tyler.

Tyler shook his hand. "Doesn't mean I like you, Kingston."

"Understood." Grey didn't need anything more from Tyler than for him to know the facts and help keep Avery safe.

Tyler glanced toward the bedrooms. "Tell Avery I'm running out to buy supplies to get her locks updated. I'll be back to install and let her know who'll be watching her six."

Grey respected her brother's ability to pull together all the safety features Avery needed. "I will."

Tyler eyed him hard. "Keep her safe."

That went without saying, but Grey replied anyway. "Will do."

Tyler headed out, slamming the door shut behind him, leaving Grey alone with the knowledge that he'd done more harm than good by returning to Avery's life. At least according to her brother. What mattered was what Avery thought, and his chances with her had always been shaky.

Now? He had no idea what he was up against. All he could do was make sure she felt the depth of his feelings for her and believed that if she was with him, she'd be protected and safe . . . and hope for the best.

Avery couldn't stand sitting around her room any longer. Ella got busy blow-drying her hair. She wouldn't discuss Tyler, just saying that Avery's brother had always been controlling, annoying, and a pain in the ass. Avery agreed, but she still sensed more brewing and couldn't begin to understand their dynamic. And why hadn't she picked up on it sooner? Meanwhile, her brother and Grey were in the other room discussing God knew what, and she'd had enough.

She swept into the room, only to find Grey staring out the window and Tyler nowhere to be seen. She took in the stiff lines of Grey's broad back, the way he braced his hands on the windowsill and looked down, lost in thought, and wondered what had been said between these two men in her life.

"Hey. Where's Tyler?"

Grey turned, his concerned gaze meeting hers. "He took off. Said to tell you he was going out to buy better locks and he'd be back to install them. He'll also be in touch about who he picks as your bodyguard."

She stiffened at the reminder of how much her life had and would change if she persisted in this relationship with Grey. No matter how short term, the tumultuous existence that followed him would become hers as well.

"Come here." Grey beckoned with a crook of his finger, and damn her, she walked over, as if pulled across the room by an invisible string.

He braced his hands on her waist, deliberately lifting her top and touching her bare skin. His palms seared like a hot brand on her skin. Her nipples tightened, her sex clenched, and need swept through her, all rational thought and concern disappearing at his touch.

"We need to talk."

Apparently she didn't have the same effect on him, and she fought through the haze of desire to regain her wits. "We do. I want to know what you and my brother discussed behind my back."

"I already told you."

She frowned. "That was what Tyler had to say. You're the one who wanted a minute with him. So . . . spill."

"That was just guy shit. We needed to get some facts straight, and we did."

"Such as?" If he wasn't going to jump her bones the way her body wanted, she intended to force honest answers from him.

"Such as the fact that I'm back in your life, and I'm not going anywhere, so he'd better get used to it and stop giving you a hard time about me."

"Oh." That statement shocked her.

The notion that Grey would take that kind of stand with Tyler took her off guard. If her brothers thought he'd made promises, they'd be even more pissed off when the inevitable happened and he left again. She bit down on her lip. Somehow she'd have to explain to the overprotective men in her family that she'd known the end result with Grey. No matter what he claimed or believed now.

She blew out a calming breath.

"*Oh?* That's all you have to say?"

She couldn't help the grin that lifted her lips. "I'm impressed that you'd take Tyler on."

He rubbed his nose against hers. "I already told you, anything for you, Very."

She melted inside and accepted that this was worth the pain and difficulty his star status would cause her. She slipped her hands around his waist, and suddenly his hard cock was nestled between her thighs. Warmth and need became a tangible thing. His breathing grew rougher, and her hips began to circle against him in a dance she couldn't control.

He let out a harsh groan that reverberated inside her, and her eyes fluttered closed as she swayed into him.

"Now *I* need an answer," he said.

She didn't know how he managed to think clearly when her panties were so wet, her sex so needy, she could barely bring herself to care that Ella was right in the next room.

Which meant whatever he wanted to know was more important to him than lifting her shirt, ripping off her shorts and panties, and thrusting inside her.

That cooled off her libido. "About what?" she asked, though now that her brain was back in control, she had a feeling she already knew.

He led her to the couch and resettled her where they'd been before, except he pulled her onto his lap. Instead of desire, nerves settled inside her.

"What did Tyler mean, asking if you had a panic attack getting past the photographers?"

She swallowed hard. She'd never admitted the truth to him back in high school because she'd been mortified by her weakness. She tried to pretend the problem didn't exist, and if she took daily medication and life stayed on a fairly even keel, it didn't. She'd tried going off the medication once before, only to have intermittent attacks occur and a low level of anxiety exist as her constant friend. Hence she'd gone back on daily maintenance medication.

She'd gotten past the embarrassment and stigma of having a generalized anxiety disorder . . . except now she was faced with telling Grey. A man who got up onstage in front of hundreds of thousands and had no such issues. She didn't know if he understood them . . . or wanted to.

He ran his hand over her back. "You can tell me anything."

"Can I?" she asked, the thoughtless words coming out.

"What's that supposed to mean?" he asked, hurt in his voice and in his stricken expression.

She sighed. "I'm sorry. It's just . . ."

Grey shook his head. "No apologies necessary. I want you to talk to me, so start at the beginning. When did you have your first panic attack?"

Avery nodded. "When I left the hospital after the bone marrow donation."

As Grey listened, she explained how the reporters had been lying in wait to question her and her mother when she'd walked out of the building.

"It was awful. Like today, except worse because I was just nine. They surrounded us like a pack of jackals and asked my mother the most embarrassing questions."

Having been on the receiving end of such questions, Grey could imagine.

"My mother held me tight against her and tried to lead me to the car, but they were so close. The bright lights, the shouting. I tried to keep it together but . . . I passed out." Even now, her cheeks flushed, and it killed Grey to think she was embarrassed to tell him.

"They're uncaring animals. Even children aren't off-limits. I hate that you went through that." He continued stroking her back, hoping he could both soothe her and keep her talking. "What happened after that?"

"I came to in an ER cubicle. My mom was frantic. It was almost a relief when they said it was a panic attack and nothing more serious."

He was afraid to ask but figured he might as well get all the ugly out at once. "And your dad? Where was he in all this?"

She froze in his arms. "With his sick daughter, Sienna, and her mother."

Grey hated Robert Dare as much, if not more, than he hated his own father. "Aww, baby. You're lucky you had your mom."

"I know. She was—is—amazing. She could have brushed it off as a one-time incident, but she didn't. Between the bone marrow and the passing out, she was worried about me. At the pediatrician's suggestion, she took me to a child psychologist, and they worked with me on calming exercises."

"Did they help?"

"Sometimes."

He figured. Because Tyler wouldn't have mentioned the panic attacks earlier if they hadn't happened again.

Grey tangled his hands in her hair and nuzzled her neck, inhaling her scent, finding comfort as much as he hoped he was instilling some in her. "Keep going," he said.

"The kids at school were brutal, so yeah. The panic attacks continued."

She curled into him, and he held on tight, wanting to never let go.

"Eventually the doctor prescribed child-safe meds. And as I got older, crowds or certain situations would trigger things again. But by then, I could take other medications, and things got under control. I'm fine."

She shrugged, clearly trying to play off the situation, something he couldn't allow. "Except you weren't fine today. Because you had to run the gauntlet of reporters just like you did back then, right?"

"I didn't pass out." She pushed herself off him and turned so she straddled his lap instead of being tucked into him. "I admit that I panicked . . . I had the symptoms, and when I got into my room, I took a Xanax for the first time in a long while, but I didn't pass out," she said with strength and conviction.

As if she wanted him to know she was strong. And he did. "Sugar, I know you handled it. I got here and you were giving your brother hell," he said with pride in his voice. "So no worries there." He pulled in a long breath, then took the conversation where he dreaded going. "The thing is, it's part of my life, not yours, and you hate it. Which means you shouldn't have to handle it. Especially when it brings back such painful memories."

His heart hurt, because he wanted her to associate him with good times, not bad. Yet he didn't know how to fix things for her. For them.

"I've seriously given this a lot of thought." She met his gaze, her eyes damp but focused on his.

He did his best to ignore the heat of her sex above his, to tamp down the uncomfortable erection caused by her position above him. Instead, he focused on her words because those moist eyes made him nervous.

"You say you're home to stay, and you believe it when you say it. But I know you, and music is in your heart. Playing to the crowd is in your soul. And eventually, normal life will get boring. Music will call to you, or the lure of the fans and touring will. And I'm not going to be the one to hold you back."

His heart, the one she claimed belonged to music, beat hard and painfully in his chest. "What are you trying to say?" Because it sounded like an ending, not the beginning he craved.

"I'm saying that I'm here with you now. I want this time with you again, except I'm older and wiser than I was before. When you go this time, I'll be more prepared. So whatever I have to deal with now, the press, the bodyguard, I'll get through it in order to have you. For however long it lasts." With tears in her eyes, she leaned close and sealed her lips over his.

Grey kissed her back, his heart in every touch of her lips and swipe of her tongue. His mind, however, was on her words. She was here because she thought this was short term. She wasn't panicking, per se, because she didn't believe he'd be part of her future. While he was trying to cement himself in the very fabric of her being, she was holding herself back, preparing for what she perceived as an inevitable end.

His heart nearly broke at the thought. He wanted to correct her, to set things straight, but doing so might be even worse. If he persisted in trying to convince her how serious he was about their future, if she thought she'd have to deal with the paparazzi and groupies long term, she might cut him off immediately. He couldn't handle losing her before he ever really had her again.

Better to stick with his original plan and make himself such a large part of her life, so indispensable to her, to show her how in love with her he really was . . . she'd be willing to put up with anything for them to be together.

And he did love her. Not the memory of her, not the girl she'd been, but the strong, beautiful woman she was now. All of her. So he'd prove to her that he was willing to give up the touring and the insanity of the road for the chance at normal. With her by his side.

He gripped her hair, tilted her head, and kissed her harder, taking control before he lost his damn mind by thinking too much. He tugged at the long strands, and she rewarded him with a shuddering moan, rocking her hips against his. Arousal built swiftly, as did the need slamming inside her, reminding them both that together, they were bigger and better than they were alone.

"Avery? Is that asshole gone?"

"Ella!" Avery squeaked, her hands pushing against his chest as she quickly rolled off him. She scooted into a sitting position while he grabbed the nearest throw pillow and covered his straining, obvious erection.

"Oh my God, I'm sorry." Her roommate spun around in a flash of light-brown hair so she could scurry back to her room.

"Don't go!" Avery said to her roommate.

Why the fuck not? Grey wondered.

"Are you sure?" Ella peered over her shoulder, giving Grey his first glimpse of her face.

"Yes. I think introductions are in order." Avery pulled herself together quicker than Grey was managing. "Ella Shaw, this is Grey Kingston."

Since he and Avery had only been together for senior year—though because of the intensity of their feelings, it felt like much longer—he hadn't met Ella in person. He had, however, heard a lot about her.

Cheeks flushed with embarrassment, she walked over and stuck out her hand. "Umm, nice to meet you."

"Likewise," he said, shifting uncomfortably and grateful for the pillow, which she clearly hadn't missed.

"God, could today get any worse?" Ella asked.

Grey shook his head, knowing he had to put the poor woman at ease. "It can only get better from here."

"He's right," Avery said. "And Tyler's gone, so that's a start for you."

That comment broke the ice, and Ella laughed, a genuine, honest giggle that Grey enjoyed, especially at Tyler's expense.

"Are you leaving for the airport soon?" Avery asked. She turned to Grey. "Ella works for a Miami-based designer who keeps her hopping with photo shoots and meetings."

"Sounds like fun."

"It actually is. I'm off to a tropical island, so no complaints here." She smiled. "Anyway, I have to finish packing. I came out to check on you, but clearly you're in good hands so . . ." She blushed at her inadvertent sexual innuendo.

Grey grinned. "Nice to meet you, Ella."

"Same here, Kingston. Take care of my girl while I'm gone," she said, pinning him with a warning glare he took seriously.

"I intend to."

As he knew from his older sister, best girlfriends were not to be underestimated. Neither was the skittish woman who wasn't taking his intentions seriously.

Chapter Seven

or Avery, the afternoon passed quickly. Grey stuck around, though they didn't discuss anything serious, just hung out like old times. He told her he liked the bright, cheerful colors she'd chosen for her apartment and he appreciated the large, comfortable furniture. She had big brothers, she reminded him, and had decorated accordingly.

Tyler returned as promised and installed a dead bolt and a new lock, necessitating two keys for entry. She refrained from rolling her eyes at him, knowing not only was this his job, but he wouldn't worry about her as much if she let him do his thing. Ella had already left for the airport, so Avery had no chance to observe her brother and her best friend again and figure out the reason for the tension she'd noticed earlier.

By the time Tyler had finished working and left for the day, it was dinnertime. "What time are we going to your parents'?" she asked.

Grey didn't answer immediately, and she walked over to where he sat on the sofa. Head bent, notepad in hand, he hummed to himself, jotting things down, lost in thought. Or in his own head.

This was Grey as she remembered from high school. Often she'd find him sitting somewhere, anywhere—the cafeteria, at a desk, outside under a tree. To the outsider, he was daydreaming, but Avery knew he was writing songs in his head, putting words to paper.

She smiled and came up behind him, wrapping her arms around his neck and snuggling her face close to his.

"Hey, sugar."

Her stomach tumbled at the endearment, and she sighed happily. Here, when they were alone, just Avery and Grey, she could pretend the outside world didn't exist. She could put her problems, *their problems*, into a little box, shut the lid, and forget for a little while. It was one of the coping strategies her first psychologist had taught her, and it came naturally now.

"Hey yourself. Tyler's gone. Yelled good-bye. You didn't even hear him go."

He winced.

"He didn't notice," she said.

"More like he didn't care, but don't worry. We've come to an understanding."

And she appreciated the effort they were both making even if Grey's was more overt than her brother's. "When do you want to go to your parents'?" she asked again.

"I figured after the day you had, you'd be exhausted and want to stay in tonight."

She frowned and walked around the sofa, sitting down beside him. "Are you trying to avoid going there?" She knew he'd have to face his mom, and sooner was better than later.

"No, I just thought you wouldn't want to deal with the paparazzi."

She closed her eyes and pulled in a deep breath. "I thought we discussed this. I'll deal with whatever I have to."

"For now," he tacked on, repeating her words from earlier. He didn't seem to like or understand why she'd said them. More like he didn't want to.

Instead of getting back on that topic, she picked up his cell phone and held it out to him. "Call your mom. Tell her we're coming over." She rose to her feet.

"Where are you going?" he asked.

"To change and get ready to leave." She didn't want to head over to his mom's in the ratty jean shorts she'd changed into to hang around for the afternoon.

"You're being bossy."

"You like me bossy." She spun and headed for the bedroom.

"I like *you*," he called out, his words ringing in her ears.

After Avery disappeared into her room, Grey pocketed the sheets of paper from the notepad he'd been writing in. It had been awhile since he'd worked on new lyrics. Being with Avery again had opened up the creative side of his brain, which had shut down after Milo's overdose. He'd channeled all the longing, the need, and desire into words that flowed onto the pages. Later he'd play with his guitar, putting them to the music floating in his head.

Being with Avery sparked his imagination. Of course, it was hell not touching her as he'd watched her help Tyler. She'd pulled her long hair into a ponytail that bounced against her back as she moved. Her sweet ass, enclosed in tight, denim shorts, had provided dirty thoughts and distractions, none of which he could act on with her brother in the room. But their banter and bickering had also helped his artistic expression. Anything she did, it seemed, brought out the best in his music.

When she finally rejoined him, she'd changed into a flowing lavender sundress with a halter top that was cinched at the waist, accentuating her sexy curves. It was a casual dress, perfect for his mom's impromptu barbecue that she'd insisted on putting together when his mom heard that not only was Grey coming over, he was bringing Avery. The excitement in her voice helped quell Grey's nerves and guilt, though he knew neither would go away completely until he apologized and explained.

For now, his focus was on his girl. He refused to think of Avery as anything less, and he whistled appreciatively as she entered the room.

She blushed, twirled, and curtsied. "Glad you like."

Nothing not to like, he thought and grinned. "Are you ready to face the lions?"

The smile on her face fell a bit, and his heart squeezed at how easily he'd taken her happiness.

"Didn't Tyler say they were gone from out front?" she asked.

Grey nodded. "They are. But one of them could be waiting on a public road, ready to follow us. They take pictures from cars too," he explained, knowing she had to understand every part of his life.

She swallowed hard. "We'll have Rick Devlin following us," she said of the bodyguard her brother had assigned to her.

She'd objected to being driven around like a pampered princess, so Grey and her brother had agreed to let Rick tail her instead. Marco often doubled as Grey's driver when going to and from venues for concerts and appearances, but he didn't think things were that intense at the moment.

They'd be fine. He didn't like the idea of needing protection, but he couldn't expect Avery to accept things easily if he didn't accept it himself.

"Good point," he said with a forced smile on his face.

"What's wrong?" Avery looked at him with concern in her pretty eyes.

Fuck that. He didn't want to make her sad or have her worry unnecessarily.

He reached out and tucked a strand of hair behind her ear. "Not a thing. I'm actually looking forward to being alone with you in the car and taking a nice drive in my Aston Martin," he said with an easier, more genuine grin.

She groaned. "Better than us slumming it in my BMW. Jeez, Grey, do you hear yourself?"

He laughed. "Only the best for you, Very. The Aston Martin it is."

A little while later, Avery gave Rick the keys to Grey's car in a discreet exchange at the building's entrance. The bodyguard pulled up front for them. He and Grey exchanged places, Avery sliding into the passenger seat—no photographers, no incident. Still, knowing they were driving his showy car, Grey wore a Mariner's cap Avery had lying around along with his sunglasses. Avery slid hers on too, and with Rick following close behind, they were on their way.

During the drive to Grey's parents', Avery chatted about Rick, who apparently had also done bodyguard duty for her sister-in-law Meg a few months ago. Grey kept an eye on him in the rearview mirror. The guy kept up with his driving and clearly had an eye on the road and another one behind him. Grey relaxed when he realized the other man would keep Avery safe when Grey wasn't around.

They pulled up to the patio home Grey had bought for his mother and stepfather in a safe, gated community. Because of Grey's fame, he'd insisted on a development with security for his mom, and they'd accepted his requirement in exchange for some of their own. Namely, no cookie-cutter complex where all homes looked alike, and the ability to do gardening on the grounds of their home themselves. No community association telling them what they could and couldn't plant, what their house had to look like, or who they had to hire for the things they couldn't do themselves.

Grey'd been so happy they had been willing to leave the not-so-safe area where he'd grown up, he'd deposited money into an account and stepped back. Too far back, he accepted now. As he parked the car, he drew in a deep breath. Time to make amends, he thought.

He looked at the immaculate, beautifully manicured lawn and shrubbery. He didn't know the name of one plant or flower they'd planted, nor did he care. But as he admired the adobe-colored house with a dark roof, the just-cut green lawn, and the pretty flowers scattered throughout, Grey acknowledged for the first time that the small home they'd chosen suited them.

Grey exited and helped Avery out of the vehicle, aware of Rick in the car, parked and idling, behind them. Avery seemed not to be bothered by her shadow, and she quickly slipped her hand into Grey's, as if she sensed how much he needed her warmth and support as they readied to see his mom and stepdad.

"It's a great community," she said. "We passed a clubhouse, and there are so many people outside walking their dogs. They must love it here."

Grey nodded. "I was just thinking how perfect it is," he said. "The right size and so immaculate outside. I bet they did it all themselves." To his surprise, he heard the pride and admiration in his voice.

Avery gave his hand a reassuring squeeze. She turned toward him, a smile on her face, so open and sweet he had to have a taste. "The house itself is so beautiful."

He braced his hands on either side of her face. "So are you," he said, his tone as gruff as the sudden surge of need. He always wanted her, but every damn time he looked into those eyes, it caught him off guard.

"Don't get started here. I have to go in and face your parents." But a pink flush of arousal stained her cheeks.

"And you don't want to be all wet and aroused when you do, huh?" he asked. Just the thought of her moist panties had him shifting uncomfortably where he stood.

"Grey!" she said, horrified, but the heady glaze in her eyes told another story. She was just as affected as him.

It had been a long day, from worrying about the press to being concerned about her refusal to be serious about them to having to face his family after so long. He couldn't think of a better way to de-stress than to lose himself in Avery. He pressed his lips hard against hers, pouring everything he had and felt into the kiss. She welcomed him, opening herself easily, his tongue claiming hers over and over.

"We have to go in," she finally murmured between breaths, but her hands weren't pushing him away; they were curling into his shirt, her nails biting into his skin.

With difficulty, he pulled away and drew in deep, calming breaths. A glance told him Rick sat discreetly in the driver's seat, ignoring his clients making out like teenagers behind the car.

"Grey!" His mother's voice brought reality crashing back around him.

He held up one finger toward her. "Just a sec," he called back.

He glanced at Avery, her eyes bright, cheeks flushed, and mouth puffy from his kiss. He swiped his finger over her damp lips. "You ready?"

"I think you should be asking yourself that question," she muttered, glancing down at his cock, straining hard against his cargo shorts.

"Yeah. Talk to me about something. Anything."

She rolled her eyes. "You started it. Now pull yourself together." With a wink and a laugh, she drew her shoulders back and headed to greet his mother.

Grey's mother met him on the front porch and hugged him tight, the familiar smell of her perfume wrapping around him. His mother had always been petite, five foot two, and when she hugged him, he towered over her. But that didn't make the strength of her hugs any less potent, and a lump formed in his throat.

"My baby boy."

Though he was slightly embarrassed at her word choice, he was also close to a complete breakdown at how easily she welcomed him home, no questions asked.

"Hi, Mom," he said, finally extricating himself from her embrace and taking her in.

She'd aged well, her skin still nearly flawless and the lines in her face minimal. Her hair was still dark, no gray, and she was clearly relaxed and happy. Life obviously agreed with her.

She grasped his hands in her weathered, work-worn ones. "Let me look at you."

Grey shot Avery an amused glance, and she grinned back at him.

"Hush," his mother said. "I'll get to her next. Humor me." She looked him over thoroughly and said, "You need to eat."

Avery burst out laughing, redrawing his mother's attention to her.

"It's so good to see you again!" His mom kissed Avery's cheek. "Thank you for bringing my boy home."

Avery's eyes grew wide, and distress flashed over her face. "No, I didn't. This was all him."

Grey's mother pinned Avery with a knowing stare, one Grey had been treated to many times growing up. "A mother knows. He came home for you."

"Mrs. Mendez," Avery began.

"Susie. You always called me by my first name, remember?"

"Susie." Avery's smile grew more genuine. "Don't believe everything you read in the papers. I didn't have anything to do with breaking up the band," she rushed to assure his mother.

As if his mom cared one bit whether or not Tangled Royal existed as long as Grey was happy.

"Those rags," she said with a dismissive wave of her hand.

"This one was reputable, but they still got it wrong," Avery said.

"Doesn't matter. I always knew you two were meant to be."

"Mom, let's go inside," Grey said before she could spook Avery any more.

As Grey walked into the house, he was struck by the memories that assaulted him. The scent was familiar, as his mom's perfume lingered. And the pictures on the walls, the pieces on the shelves, the furniture in the living room were all equally familiar. They'd allowed him to buy the house, but they'd kept the old furniture. Some of the pieces were refurbished, but Ricardo always had a talented hand, and Grey felt certain he'd done the work himself.

Instead of frustration, a sense of pride welled up in him for both his mom and stepdad. "Is Ricardo home?"

"He's out back. Why don't you go help him with the grill, and Avery and I will go into the kitchen." Grey glanced at Avery, but she was already following his mother into the kitchen.

Grey found his stepfather outside on the patio.

"Grey!" Ricardo, a tall, slender man with salt-and-pepper hair, stepped over and pulled him into a one-armed hug, patting him on the back. "It's good to see you."

"Same," Grey said.

"Your mother is over the moon. She's so happy you're here."

Grey did his best not to squirm. Though he knew his stepdad wasn't trying to make him feel bad or uncomfortable, he did. There were still things that needed to be said between them.

"So tell me how things are going for you," Ricardo said. "Is the band really splitting up?"

Grey nodded. "We reached the end. It's hard to explain, but we're all ready to do our own thing."

Ricardo reached into a cooler and pulled out two beers, handing one to Grey. They popped the tops, and he took a long, cool drink.

"I can understand that. You should be proud though. You went out and accomplished your dream. Not many people can say they did that."

Warmth filled Grey's chest as Ricardo gave him the words his own father had always denied him. "Thank you," he said, infusing his tone with emotion and meaning. "So how are you? How's Mom?"

"Living the good life, thanks to you." He gestured to the backyard with the nice-size patio, a pool on the side with a spa. Over to the side, there was a barbecue built into a stone wall. "Put this in myself," he said with pride.

Grey grinned. "The house looks fantastic."

"I'm glad you pushed us to move. Your mother is so much happier here. Good neighborhood, nice friends. Thank you," he said, not for the first time.

Grey shook his head. "Don't. Don't thank me. I'm glad you're happy. It's all I wanted, but back then I wanted . . ." He trailed off, the words sticking in his throat.

Ricardo put a weathered hand on Grey's shoulder. "No need, son."

"There's every need." Grey's voice caught, the word *son* still echoing in his head. "Back then, I wanted you to be different. I didn't want you to be a janitor. I wanted you to have aspirations and dreams."

"Nothing wrong with wanting more," the older man said. "I was happy with a decent job that fed my family, but I respect what you accomplished."

He didn't get it. "I was embarrassed," Grey said, needing to say the words, to purge them and the awful feelings from his brain. "I acted and treated you like my father treated me, and that's unforgiveable."

Ricardo led him to a set of chairs, and they settled in. "When I met your mother, you were an angry, hurting boy. You had good reason. I don't imagine it was easy for you to go to school while your stepfather cleaned up everyone's messes. Your reaction was normal for a teenager. Even more normal for one whose father messed up his head."

"Even later, when I insisted you move, I wanted you to live where I thought you should. I didn't understand or respect who you were or what you wanted."

"You wanted to make our lives better. How can I fault you for that?"

"How can you not? Worse, I haven't been home in too long."

Ricardo leaned back in his chair, his long, tanned legs stretched in front of him. "You're here now, yes? And you see what's really important in life?"

Grey inclined his head. "I hope so."

"Then your mother and I did our jobs. What we instilled in you back then, what you rejected because you didn't understand, you now accept. With age comes wisdom. Only by living life can you figure out what's truly important."

"Do you see why I fell in love with this man?"

His mother's voice took Grey by surprise. He'd been so focused on listening to Ricardo's wise words he hadn't heard the women join them. He glanced at Avery and his mom, wondering how much they'd heard. From the dampness in his mother's eyes, too much. And maybe enough.

"You chose well, Mom," Grey said to her for the first time.

"I know." She smiled and kissed her husband's cheek. "There's something to be said about marrying for love," Susie said. "And learning from past mistakes. Can we move on and just enjoy our day together?" she asked.

Grey nodded, knowing he'd learned so much from these two people in front of him and hoping he could use it to make his life as happy as theirs obviously was.

He rose and walked over to Avery, slipping his hand into her smaller, softer one. "Everything good?"

She nodded. "Your mom's amazing. And that kitchen? Grey! It's so great. State of the art."

"It's the one thing she let me gut and do from scratch in the house. She loves to cook."

"Well, you should see what she has ready to put on the grill. You'd think she had a week's notice that we were coming. And the desserts? To die for."

He grinned. "That's my mom."

The rest of the evening passed quickly. They reminisced about Avery and Grey in high school, bringing him back to the reason he'd returned home—the woman who was currently helping his mother bring dishes into the kitchen from the patio, where they'd eaten dinner. In the short time he'd been back, he'd realized Avery still understood him in ways no one else did. She saw the fragile boy beneath the rock star persona and supported him. That was what Avery meant to him, did for him.

The chemistry was a bonus and had only grown stronger over the years. Watching her in that sexy dress, her hips swaying as she walked, her cleavage covered due to the higher halter but hints of her full breasts teasing him beneath the material, Grey decided family time was over.

"We need to get going," Grey said, rising to his feet.

"Grey! I haven't finished helping your mom yet." Avery shot him a chiding gaze that only served to make him hotter.

"You two go. We're finished here," his mother said.

Glancing at the mostly cleaned table, Avery nodded. "If you're sure."

"You two have better things to do than hang out with the old folks. I'm just so happy you came by."

"And I'll come again, Mom. I promise." He rose and hugged his mother tight. "I love you, Mom."

"I love you too."

Grey said good-bye to his stepfather, and Avery made her rounds too. Finally, they were in the car, driving home.

"Things went well, yes?" Avery asked.

"Very." Although he and his mother hadn't had an in-depth conversation, she'd heard what he'd said to Ricardo, and in his heart, Grey knew she understood how he felt.

"Someone was in a hurry to leave though." Avery turned her head, and he caught her gaze for a moment before returning his focus to the road.

"And you wonder why?" He placed a hand on her knee and inched his fingers up her silken skin, reaching slowly higher until he encountered lace.

He wondered what color it was, and he accelerated, wanting to find out faster.

"Grey," she said, her attempt at reprimanding him turning into a moan as his fingers slid over her sex, and he discovered her panties were already damp.

"Problem, sugar?" he asked, stroking the lace covering her slick, hot flesh, and his cock jumped inside his shorts.

"You need to drive," she said, her voice hoarse with desire.

He swallowed a moan of his own. "Good thing for you I can do two things at once. And do them both well."

His gaze remained on the road, but the rest of his senses were attuned to her. He pressed his thumb over her clit, and her thighs parted, giving him better access.

"Do you want to know why I left so quickly?" He didn't give her a chance to respond. "I'll tell you. Because I watched you all night, so sweet and pretty as you helped my mom, and all I could think about was messing up your hair with my hands, hiking up that dress, and taking you hard and fast. You want that too, don't you?"

She arched her hips, her pussy thrusting against his fingers, so needy.

He wanted her at his place, and that's where he was headed, but first he had to hear her come. He gripped the wheel with one hand, his teeth clenched so hard his jaw ached.

With his free hand, he slid his fingers beneath her panties and encountered bare flesh. "Fuck, you're wet for me." He stroked her sex, lubricating his fingers, gliding back and forth over her clit.

He caught sight of his exit and managed to take the correct one, her heavy breathing beating a rapid cadence in his ear. He toyed with the tiny bud, alternating between tweaking it between his thumb and forefinger and soothing it with slick strokes.

"Grey, God, harder, so close. So close." Her hips bucked rapidly against him, and she grabbed his wrist, shoving his hand hard against her sex.

She was frantic, and he couldn't focus. Couldn't get her off without killing them both. He didn't know what the fuck he'd been thinking. He'd just needed to feel her so damned bad.

"Hang on." He swore and removed his hand.

She whimpered and began to stroke herself with no help from him. Fuck that. "Do not come without me," he ordered.

"Seriously?" Her gaze met his, a heady mixture of disbelief and desire filling the depths.

"Yes," he bit out, pulling over to the side of the road not far from his apartment.

She was still stroking herself when he shoved the gearshift into park, removed his seat belt, and maneuvered his body closer so he had more room, more leverage.

"Hands on either side of your lap," he said in his deepest, most commanding tone.

She balled her hands into fists at her sides, and he relaxed a bit.

He leaned across the console and kissed her hard, at the same time sliding her panties down to her knees. He pushed two fingers inside her tight channel, gliding in and out, pressing hard on her clit with his thumb.

Her body, already on the edge, convulsed immediately, gripping his fingers as she came. "Grey," she cried out and rode out her climax, a sight so fucking beautiful it was seared in his memory forever.

When she fell back against the seat, limp and sated, he pulled her dress down, covering her sex. With her sweet pussy out of view, he hoped he'd make it home without dying first. He'd broken into a sweat himself and pushed his hand hard against his cock to calm himself down before he could even think of driving again.

Without warning, a knock sounded, and both he and Avery jumped in surprise. He turned to see Rick gesturing for him to roll down the window. He'd forgotten about their shadow, and clearly Avery had as well.

Grey shot her a wry glance, made sure she really was covered up, and hit the window button. "Hey, man."

Rick rested an arm on the top of the car and leaned down to look inside. "Just making sure everything's okay here."

"We're good. We just had something to discuss."

Rick treated him to a knowing smirk. "Well, you might want to keep moving before someone notices you."

"Right," Grey muttered. "You're off duty till morning," he informed the man.

Rick tapped the top of the car and headed back to his vehicle.

"Oh my God," Avery said in a horrified moan. "If he'd come over a few seconds sooner . . ."

At the thought of another man seeing Avery undressed, Grey's protective instincts rose to the surface. "And that's another good reason to head home." Along with his aching cock and the driving need to bury himself deep inside Avery as soon as humanly possible.

Chapter Eight

Avery normally wasn't a multiorgasm girl, so she was surprised she was aroused again by the time they reached Grey's apartment. Of course, she'd immediately noticed how hard he was from giving her pleasure, and she wanted to reciprocate. She wanted to hold his hard, stiff length in her hands and taste his cock with her mouth. She didn't think she'd ever had these thoughts about a man before, and for sure they'd never aroused her to the point of needing to come again so soon.

Grey was about to turn into the parking garage and waved as Rick passed them, his job for the night complete. Grey parked in the underground garage. He came around to her side before she could even get her door open.

"I'm not sure I can wait much longer," he said, and pulled her out of the car.

"Grey!"

He lifted her into his arms and strode to the elevator. The private elevator that led directly to his floor. She wrapped her arms around his neck and held on.

"You're spoiling me," she murmured. "I mean, a girl could get used to this kind of treatment."

"That's the point."

She rested her chin on his shoulder, her cheek against his, and blocked out his words. Short term. She couldn't allow herself to get attached to her musician.

Not hers. "God."

"What's wrong?" he asked as the elevator opened and he let them into the apartment, kicking the door shut behind them.

She slid down his hard, toned body, her breasts and nipples feeling every hard ridge and plane of his chest. Her fingers itched to touch bare skin. Indulging her desire, she pulled up his shirt and slid her hands along his flat stomach and six-pack abs.

He groaned, his body shaking beneath her touch, and a thrill slid through her. She didn't have much experience, and a lot of it came from Grey, so the knowledge that she could make him tremble more now than years before did things to her female ego. She scraped her nails up his chest until she reached his nipples, drawing her fingers over the distended peaks.

"Are you trying to push me over the edge?" he asked, leaning forward and nipping her on the ear.

She moaned and arched into him. "Maybe."

"Maybe it's time to turn the tables." He pulled her dress up and over her head, leaving her dressed in flimsy panties and a barely there bra.

His hot gaze raked over her, admiration settling over his handsome face. "Look at you," he muttered, sliding a hand beneath her hair, around her neck, and pulling her in for a scorching kiss.

His tongue tangled with hers, while at the same time, he backed her up until her legs hit the couch. She toppled backward onto the soft cushions. She adjusted herself, letting her sandals fall to the floor.

She kept her gaze on his, watching his every movement. He stripped off his shirt and kicked off his shoes. Pulled a condom from inside his wallet before removing his shorts, taking his boxer briefs with them. Finally he stood before her, his naked body a thing of beauty.

Without thought, she unhooked the front clasp of her bra, extricating her arms from the straps and freeing her aching breasts for his viewing pleasure. He stared down at her, green eyes glittering with arousal, his erection strong, thick, and big, making her mouth water and her body moisten with desire.

"I still can't believe we're here. Together," she said, voicing the thought she couldn't get out of her head.

He placed the condom on the end table and came down over her, his hard cock sliding over her sex, causing a rush of need to wash over her.

"It's us," he assured her.

She moaned, her clit pulsing and her body clenching with the desire to be filled by him.

"Grey, I need you." She scored her nails over his back, hoping to entice him into moving faster. Sure enough, he arched his hips, thrusting against her, causing another delicious wave of longing to toss her around but not take her over.

"You want to run the show?" he asked, sitting up suddenly and pulling her with him. He grasped her hips and shifted her around until she straddled him, her knees on either side of his muscular thighs. "Grab the condom."

Her heart beat out a rapid rhythm, but she did as he asked and plucked the foil packet from the table.

"Now open it and slide it on me," he instructed, his voice gravelly.

"I've never done that before." But excitement buzzed in her veins because she wanted to do it with him.

"Good." Grey brushed a thumb over her cheek, as amazed as she was that they were together. He wanted to memorize every second, make it last, keep her here with him forever. He'd been her first ever, and damn but he wanted to be her last.

She curled her soft fingers around his aching shaft, and he held himself still, watching as she bit the inside of her cheek and ripped open the package, removing the condom. Precum had already formed on the head of his cock, and he clenched his jaw and gripped her hips harder, all in an effort not to embarrass himself by coming too soon.

His hold on his body was a tenuous one. Unaware of his strain, she rolled the condom over him, moving slowly, carefully, the glide of her fingers a tease he could barely withstand until, finally, she reached the base of his shaft.

"Done!" she said, her voice filled with pride.

She was such a mixture of innocent and sensual woman, was it any wonder he found her so fucking special?

"Now ride me, sugar," he said tightly, hoping he made it past the first grip of her pussy before exploding.

"Can't say I've ever done *that* before either, but I'm game to try." With a sexy smile on her face, Avery placed her delicate hands on his shoulders and raised herself up on her knees.

Her wet heat hovered over the head of his cock, and he gripped the base until his shaft nudged its way inside her. At the first clasp of her pussy, sweat broke out on his skin. She moved herself up and down until she was able to slide all the way home, cushioning him inside her completely.

"Oh my God," she said on a groan. "You feel . . . this is . . ."

"Intense," he said, completing her sentence in the only way he could. His dick was on fire as she squeezed him in her narrow passage. If she didn't move soon, he might die.

"Incredible," she murmured, leaning forward and sliding her lips over his.

The kiss broke open a dam between them, and he arched up into her at the same time she rocked back and forth, her snug pussy contracting around him until he couldn't see, breathe, hear, think, or feel anything but her. How could he when she was grinding her sex into him and her breasts were gliding against his chest, her tight, hard nipples grazing his skin?

He gripped her hair, tilted her head, and ran his tongue along her neck, nipping at her flesh with his teeth. She whimpered at the tiny bites and began to fuck him harder, raising and lowering her hips until he was meeting her moves with pitched thrusts of his own.

"Harder, Grey, please!" She dug her nails into his shoulders, and with each downward plunge, she arched her sex forward, seeking more friction.

He slipped his hand between their bodies, his fingertips coming into contact with her clit. He massaged her moisture around the distended bud with determined circles until her breath came in shorter gasps, her rocking motions became less fluid and more jerky as she chased her climax.

He was damned close himself, flashes of heat singeing him, but he wasn't coming without her. He wanted to watch, knowing that seeing her go off would send him over the edge right after her.

"Come for me, sugar." He rubbed her clit harder.

She clenched around his cock, her hips rocking against his. "Oh God, Grey!" She cried out his name, began chanting it as she came, her entire body a writhing mass of need and want. And when she wrapped her arms around his neck and rocked herself into him, she was still coming, still whispering his name. It triggered his own release as he pumped his hips upward, relieving himself of hot, sizzling come.

Avery held him tight as he came, waiting until he collapsed beneath her before she did the same. He wrapped his arms around her, knowing that he'd finally gotten it right. He'd come home.

Avery woke up and immediately realized she was in a Grey's bed. She looked over and didn't see Grey, so she climbed out of bed and wrapped an afghan around herself before heading out of the room. She found Grey in the kitchen, drinking a glass of water. Unlike her, he was nude and clearly not bothered by that fact.

Neither was she. Looking at him was something she could do every day or night.

"Everything okay?" she asked.

"Yeah. I was just thirsty." He held out the glass. "Want some?"

"No thanks. I'll meet you back in the bedroom."

She turned to go, and he snagged her around the waist and spun her to face him. "Now that you're awake, I'm hungry too."

She blinked up at him, her eyes adjusting more in the dark room. "You are, hmm?"

"For you, pretty girl," he said, sealing his lips over hers.

She melted into him, winding her arms around his neck and kissing him back. The blanket fell to the floor, and she was skin to skin, his hard erection pressing against her belly, causing a rush of liquid to pool between her thighs.

"Bed," he said between kisses.

She wasn't going to argue, and when he lifted her, she wrapped her legs around his waist and let him carry her into the bedroom. He deposited her in the center of the bed and crawled down her body. Starting at her navel, he pressed a soft kiss there, moving lower, licking and nuzzling his way down her stomach. Her skin quivered, and arousal thrummed in her veins, her sex feeling needy and swollen as he teased her. He slid his tongue lower, tasting her slick outer lips, suckling first one, then the other into his mouth.

She moaned and gripped the blanket, writhing beneath him on the mattress, her inflamed body needing more than the leisurely laps of his tongue. As if sensing she was at her limit, he slid one long finger inside her, keeping his thumb pressed hard on her clit.

"Grey!" She arched her hips, and he blew a stream of warm air over her wet sex before adding a second finger.

"Do you feel me, sugar?"

"Yes." Her hips bucked upward, pulling his fingers deeper.

"Damn, you feel good. So hot and wet."

His words sent her soaring, taking her out of her head. He pumped in and out, spreading her wider, taking her higher. And when he sucked her clit into his mouth, she shattered, his hard fingers bringing her up and over, waves of pleasure soaring through her body over and over.

At the sound of ripping foil, she opened her eyes and welcomed Grey as he came over her and thrust into her wet sheath. She'd have thought she was finished, that it was his turn, but he was so thick, so hard, he hit a spot inside her that she'd never felt before.

"So good," she said, arching up, taking more of him.

"The best," he said, staring into her eyes as if he could consume her whole.

Jaw set, he began a steady pumping of his hips, each slam inside her awakening nerve endings that caused sparks of heat and light to wash over her as another orgasm, stronger and more powerful than the first, took hold. She lost herself in sensation, in waves of spectacular feeling, her climax consuming her. He followed her over, coming with a shout and a loud groan, collapsing against her in a sweaty, male heap.

She wrapped her arms around him and held on, knowing it was too late for her heart, the thought scaring her to death. They shared a quick late-night shower before crawling back into bed. Grey immediately fell into a deep sleep, Avery following quickly after.

Avery woke up to find her heart racing way too fast. A quick glance told her Grey still slept. He lay close. In fact she'd been cuddled into him for most of the night, his body heat comforting her. She wasn't used to sleeping with a man, yet she'd slept well. Another reason for her sudden anxiety—she was getting too attached.

She drew a deep breath in, holding it before blowing it out, counting down slowly the way she'd been taught to calm her galloping pulse and thoughts. It had been a long time since she'd woken up to pure panic, but she wasn't surprised she'd done so now. Last night had been intense, to the point where her emotions had been so big and overwhelming they'd threatened to choke her. Certainly they'd brought her to the verge of tears.

They were good tears, coming because she and Grey had *made love*, but the beauty of that had taken her off guard and threatened the walls she'd built to keep herself safe.

Despite her intentions to be smart and careful, she'd allowed herself to get into a situation that was bound to hurt her in the end.

She stared at his sleeping form for a little while longer, studying his beloved face, as if she hadn't already committed it to memory years before. She took in the changes, the adult version, and she didn't see the musician the world loved; she only viewed the man she loved.

Loved.

That sent her thoughts into another spiral. She didn't want to walk away from Grey until she had to, but she needed some distance in order to regain perspective. She wouldn't find it in his bed, watching him sleep.

The covers fell to his waist, revealing his bare chest with a liberal sprinkling of dark hair. She curled her fingers into a fist in order to resist the urge to run her hands over his skin. She couldn't risk waking him, because she needed to sneak out. When he asked later, she'd explain that she'd had work to do on her prom plans and on her blog, but the fact was she needed to get away.

She slipped out of bed, boxing up the *L* word that would surely wreak havoc on her life and tucking it away. She couldn't think about loving Grey, because he *was* the musician the world adored.

And that was that.

A little while later, she dressed in last night's clothes and texted Rick to pick her up in front of Grey's building. She had a list of things piling up in her head, and she knew she could keep herself busy with work. She didn't have to dwell on the fact that she'd bailed on Grey and would have to deal with him later.

Rick left her to her thoughts on the ride home, for which she was grateful. He pulled into a spot in front of her building and met her outside her side of the car.

Like most of the men who worked for her brothers, Rick was former military. He was tall, with big muscles, cropped dark hair, and a commanding demeanor. But because Avery knew him, she was never intimidated.

"Thanks, Rick," she said, looking up at him, unable to see his eyes thanks to his aviators. "I can walk myself up."

"Sorry, but I'm taking you to your door. Boss's orders."

Avery bit back a retort about what his boss could do with those orders and smiled at the man who was just doing his job. "Then let's go."

They made their way to her apartment, no paparazzi or strange person in sight. "See? Nobody's here, outside or in," she said as they walked down the hall to her door.

"You never know where they'll pop up, so it's better to be safe than sorry," Rick said. "Do you have your keys?"

She dug into her purse as she walked, realizing as she always did when she looked for something in the abyss that she really ought to carry a smaller bag. Unfortunately she liked knowing she had all sorts of items on hand: wallet, lip gloss, nail file, tissues, mirror, iPad mini, phone, water bottle, among other things. Just in case.

"Son of a bitch," Rick said in a harsh tone that had Avery looking up from her search.

Before she could focus on what was wrong, he braced his hands on her shoulders and pushed her against the wall protectively. "Wait here."

Her heart rate picked up speed. "What's wrong?" she asked Rick, but he was already on his cell, barking orders that included, "Problem. Call 911 and get over here now."

She stepped around him, determined to see what had him so thrown. She got a glimpse of her front door, where the words *whore, slut,* and one other she couldn't bring herself to even think about were scrawled in bright red. And the pièce de résistance: a note taped to the door with words printed on it—*Grey is mine. Break up or die.*

She gasped, a combination of horror and outrage filling her.

"Stay back," Rick said and yanked her behind him.

"Too late," she muttered, her stomach churning at the thought that someone had gotten so close to her apartment. And if she'd been inside, they'd have gotten that close to *her.*

Grey woke up and immediately knew he was alone. The warm body that had been beside him all night was gone, and his gut told him he wouldn't find her anywhere in his apartment. He ran his hand over his eyes and groaned.

He'd wanted to spend a leisurely morning eating break-fast in bed, showing her the apartment next door and his plans for a soundproof studio and a place to write and work. Instead, he had Avery's scent and the lingering smell of sex surrounding him, and he was sporting wood, but the woman he wanted in his arms was nowhere to be found.

He didn't doubt for one minute that she'd panicked and run. He was disappointed but not discouraged. He even understood. Nothing about last night had been sim-ple or easy. Everything between them had been serious and emotional.

He'd originally thought he was fighting insecurities instilled in her by a selfish, neglectful parent and the dam-age he himself had done by leaving and not staying in touch. Now he knew there were real psychological issues at work, anxiety she couldn't always control. All he could do was pro-vide a steady presence and trust she'd work through things inside her head. If there was one person he was okay trust-ing in, it was Avery. Now *she* had to do the same.

He dressed and headed over to see her, surprised to find her door open and her brother's raised voice from inside.

"You damn well are moving in with me, Ian and Riley, or Scott and Meg for the time being."

"Agreed," another male voice said. "And you can break up with that asshole who's bringing all sorts of trouble to your door."

The door, Grey noticed now, that had crude insults scrawled on the front. His stomach churned at the sight.

"You both need to back off now," Avery yelled at them, and Grey figured the second voice was another brother getting protective.

He was equally pissed at how they spoke to Avery, made decisions for her, and wanted to cut him out of her life. He pushed the door open and stormed inside.

"Grey!" Avery met his gaze, clearly startled to see him in her apartment.

"Fuck. Haven't you done enough?" Scott asked. He stood beside Tyler, both similar in looks with their dark hair and Dare-sibling violet eye color.

Grey met the man's angry stare head on. Grey counted himself lucky that he was spared Ian's presence, because of all the brothers, he was the most volatile. Not that Grey couldn't handle him, and would for Avery, but these two were enough for now.

"I'd say you're the one who's done enough." Grey slammed the door shut behind him. "Don't you think your sister can make her own decisions? She wants to be with me, and I sure as hell intend to be with her. So how about we agree to keep her safe and stop trying to cut me out of the picture? Because I won't tolerate it."

Both brothers eyed him warily.

"And just how do you propose to keep her safe when you're the one bringing the crazies to her door?" Scott asked.

Avery stepped up beside him, but she didn't get close or give him any real indication of her feelings. He couldn't imagine the fear and panic she must be holding inside. He wanted to pull her tight against him and promise her everything would be all right, but she didn't seem to want the intimacy they'd already established. He wasn't sure if she was keeping her physical and emotional distance because of her brothers or if she was pulling away all on her own.

"Can we all just calm down?" she asked.

Scott shoved his hands into his pants pockets. "Fine. Any idea what we're dealing with?" Scott asked, obviously focusing on something he could control.

Grey met Tyler's gaze. The other man already knew about the Emerald threat, and now they'd have to tell Avery. He ran a hand through his hair, frustrated at how something seemed to thwart him every time he got close to her.

Avery caught the knowing look between Grey and her brother. "What's going on?" she asked, realizing at once they were hiding something from her.

"I got a letter from an obsessed fan. She made some noises about me belonging to her and making sure you knew that, but since you'd just dealt with the paparazzi and you had a bodyguard anyway, I didn't want to add to your stress." He winced as he spoke, obviously realizing his mistake.

"I'm assuming you knew?" She glared at Tyler. "And you both decided to keep it from me?" she asked, her anger and hurt building. "What? You didn't think I could handle the truth?"

Grey reached for her, but she stepped away. He flinched at her withdrawal, but she couldn't let herself care.

"More like he knew you'd come to your senses and run the other way," Scott muttered.

"Shut up!" she and Grey said at the same time.

Avery blew out a frustrated breath. More than her overbearing brothers, Grey needed to understand that while she might have an anxiety disorder, she was fully capable of handling any news that came her way. She might not like it, and he might not appreciate how she chose to deal with things, but it was her choice to make.

"I need to make sure your landlord puts a security system on the front door to the building," Tyler said.

Avery knew that was his way of diffusing the tense situation. "Fine."

"Doesn't change the fact that you can't stay here now," her brother went on. "Even with security, anyone can walk in right behind someone with a key card. It's not a fail-safe."

"A public breakup would be a good fail-safe," Scott muttered.

Grey stepped forward, and Avery braced a hand on his chest, stopping him from going after her brother.

"Go home," she said over her shoulder to her siblings. "Grey and I need to talk."

"But—"

"I have Rick sitting in his car," she reminded them. "He was with me when I saw the door, so I was never in any danger. And the police were already here, a report's been filed, and they dusted for prints. There's nothing more you two can do."

It took more arguing and also longer than she would have liked, but she finally herded her brothers out the door, locking up behind them.

She pulled on her reserve strength and turned to Grey. Concern flashed in his green eyes, and though she couldn't read his mind, she knew for sure he was guilt-ridden that she was a virtual prisoner thanks to his life, confused at why she'd bailed on him this morning, and worried about what this new turn of events meant for them.

She wished she had answers for him, but she was just as confused, just as uncertain.

"Come here." He held out his arms.

Unable to resist, she stepped forward and walked straight into his embrace, burying her face in his soft T-shirt and inhaling his familiar scent. He wrapped his arms around her tight and held on. She wished it were just the two of them, that the outside world and all her worries would disappear. But that wasn't reality. It never had been. In her life, the outside world always intruded; something new always popped up to ruin the status quo in which she'd found a safe haven.

When she finally pulled free, he led her to the couch, and they sat down. He faced her, holding her hands in his. "Your brother is right about one thing. I'm the one who brought all this shit to your door. I can leave and make it all go away."

"No!" She'd come home needing time to think. She hadn't counted on the turmoil that had waited for her here, and she hadn't yet had a moment to put her thoughts together, but she knew one thing. Panic struck her at the thought of losing him before she was ready.

His shoulders dropped in relief. "Good. I'd do anything to keep you safe, and I'd go if you asked me to . . . but that's the last thing I want."

"I don't want that either," she whispered.

"Then why did you leave without waking me?" His rough fingers stroked her skin.

She'd hoped for more time before having to answer this question. "Last night was intense," she admitted. "I'm feeling things that I can't afford to let myself feel for you."

He nodded, and she knew he understood without her having to explain more.

"Your brothers are right. You shouldn't be alone here," he said, changing the subject. "I understand if you want to stay with them."

"Oh, hell no," she said, shuddering at the thought. "They'd drive me mad. It would be like being in a cage. Their eyes would be on me constantly. And since I don't know what kind of threat this really is, I don't want to move in with my mom or sisters and bring trouble their way."

He squeezed her hands tighter. "Move in with me then."

"What?" she asked, shock racing through her.

"Move in with me." He met her gaze, his expression as serious as she'd ever seen it. "I'm not going to say something stupid like you can stay in the guest room, because we both know that's not happening. But if you really want your space, you can stay in the apartment across the hall. Though let me go on record as saying that's not my first choice."

She blinked, trying to take in all the information he was giving her. "You own that apartment too?"

He nodded. "I live in Rep's old place. The other one was Lola's—that's how they met. I bought both, knowing I wanted to build a soundproof studio, where I can work without bothering anyone."

He'd really planned out this notion of living in Miami. More so than she'd originally thought. "I had no idea."

"I was going to explain all this to you this morning. I wanted to have breakfast and show you the layout and plans."

"But I left."

He shrugged. "We can still have breakfast now, and I can show you the apartment later?"

Her head was swimming with information and with confusion. She wouldn't feel safe sleeping in her apartment knowing someone was out there . . . in a sense, stalking her. But was she ready to move in with Grey, even temporarily? And if so, should she move into his place or across the hall?

She blew out a deep breath and said the only thing that came to mind. "Breakfast sounds like a really good idea right now."

He laughed, knowing she was avoiding any decisions. "French toast or pancakes? Either is my specialty." And obviously, he would let her take her time deciding.

She grinned. "French toast. That's all I have the ingredients for."

He leaned in and kissed her lips. "Then we go take a tour of my place."

"Only if, while we eat, you tell me about this e-mail you received . . . and who you think is behind it."

The happy light in his eyes dimmed at the reminder, and he hesitated before answering. "Fine."

"And as long as you promise no more secrets between us."

"Okay," he said, faster and with more ease.

She wasn't anywhere close to making a decision. In fact, she still wanted some space and time before doing anything, especially now that the stakes were higher than just an emotional tizzy over falling in love. But she also knew she couldn't walk away from him yet.

She was afraid she would never be able to make that break. And waiting for him to be the one to ultimately walk away left her in an even bigger panic. So she'd eat breakfast and see his apartment and plans. Then she'd take a break and go visit with her mom or Olivia and get some much-needed perspective before making any huge decisions. Like whether or not to move in with Grey.

Chapter Nine

After a breakfast of French toast and maple syrup and then cleanup, which he also insisted on doing, Grey took Avery back to his place. His heart was racing, well aware that she hadn't made a decision about moving in with him, however temporarily. And also aware that every little thing that happened between them could change her mind. It was nerve-racking, but he accepted it. Told himself that the cops would connect Emerald to the vandalism, that his intended lifestyle would get boring for the press, the paparazzi, and the fans, and that they could live a normal life.

He hoped he wasn't deluding himself.

After they took the elevator to his floor, he decided to walk her through Lola's old place first. He unlocked the door and gestured for her to enter.

"As you can see, it has the same layout as my apartment, but the decor is much different." Where he had dark wood accents, courtesy of the furniture Rep had left behind, Lola's was pops of color and huge pieces of comic book–inspired artwork on the walls.

"Oh my God! Is that . . . Superman and Wonder Woman kissing in midair?" Avery asked, delighted at the sight.

"Yeah. And it'll be the first thing to go when we start work in here," he muttered.

She laughed. "This is so great!"

He rolled his eyes and went on to explain the plans for turning this apartment into a studio. She listened intently, and he had the distinct sense she could see and appreciate his vision.

"And this is . . . was Lola's bedroom. She left me with sheets and the bedspread so that if any of our friends visited, I wouldn't have to deal with buying stuff. So if you weren't ready to move in with me, you could stay here until it was safe for you to go home." He tried to keep the disappointment out of his voice, knowing she had to come to him willingly, not because the situation was forced on her.

Avery walked inside and looked around the also brightly decorated room. "Lola does love primary colors," Avery mused. "My bright colors are pale compared to hers."

He shoved his hands into his pants pockets and waited for her to finish peeking into the master bath.

"Grey, I don't know what I want to do yet."

He nodded in understanding, frustrated but determined not to let it show.

"Want to head next door?" he asked.

She bit her bottom lip, and he knew he wasn't going to like what came next. "I asked Rick to take me to meet up with Olivia. She's done a lot of fundraising for the Thunder, and I figured she'd have some ideas to help me get up and running with the prom for the kids. And Sienna wants to help, so she's going to join us," she said of her half sister, whose life Avery had saved. Of course it made sense that Sienna would want to join in on the effort to help the kids.

Grey managed an easy shrug. "I have work to do anyway. I got a call from Chloe Mandrake, the lead singer of Night Madness. She wants to talk about me writing for their next album."

"Grey, that's great!" Avery's eyes sparkled with delight at the news.

"She said she loved the work I did with Alden Mills on the Christmas album last year."

Mills was a reclusive musician renowned for his time with Beyond the Lights, a band from the early seventies whose fame nearly matched the Beatles. They hadn't lasted long but had had a major impact on anyone in the music scene, old or new. And when he'd contacted Grey through Simon and requested him for his final solo album, a combination of old work and new lyrics, Grey had jumped at the chance.

As it turned out, Alden had been extremely ill, and Grey had done the bulk of the writing on the final songs, allowing joint credit publicly. All Grey had wanted was the opportunity to work and learn from the man's genius. He'd been in awe of the older man, and they'd kept in touch until his death a few months ago.

"Aren't you excited?" Avery asked.

"It's a cool next step," he said, though his thrill didn't match Avery's, his mood tempered by the feeling that she was deliberately keeping her distance.

Then again, she had legitimate work to do, and he was being a selfish ass, wanting to keep her close.

"How about we meet back here for dinner? I'm in the mood for seafood," he said, coming up with an idea to wine and dine her on the terrace later.

"I'd like that," she said, stepping closer and wrapping her arms around his neck. Her touch eased the tension that had been building all morning.

"I don't want my life to screw up yours," he told her.

"I know it's a part of you." She drew a deep breath. "And I'm really trying to deal with it."

He knew that. He just didn't know what or who was waiting around the corner to fuck with their happiness.

He dipped his head and slid his lips over hers, unable to stop with one kiss. He smelled his shower gel and shampoo from the night before, lingering. And although he missed her sexy vanilla scent, knowing she was walking around with *his* scent on her did something to him, and a low growl escaped from the back of his throat.

She broke the kiss and slid her lips down his neck, nuzzling his skin and licking him there. He picked her up and had her back against the wall in a heartbeat. She didn't complain, so he lifted her skirt and cupped her sex in his hand, her heat, her dampness seeping into his flesh and turning him on beyond anything he'd felt before.

He wanted to own her. To claim and possess her, to brand her so when she walked out that door, she wouldn't just smell like him, she'd belong to him. And come back to him.

She rocked into his hand, and he yanked at her panties, tearing at the lace until it ripped and the scrap went flying across the room.

She pulled at his shirt and eased her hands beneath, scraping her nails against his nipples, a favorite play of hers, one that drove him mad.

He bit back a groan and slid two fingers into her tight channel. "Fuck, sugar, you're wet for me."

She whimpered and tilted her hips forward. He pumped his fingers in and out, enjoying the sounds escaping from her throat. Sex wasn't the problem between them, and he wasn't above using whatever did work to bind her to him and make her remember where she belonged.

With each thrust, he curled his fingers against the soft, fleshy part of her that clearly had her grinding against him and begging for more.

"You, Grey, I need you."

"Need you too." He stepped away from her only long enough to shove his jeans down his legs, glad he'd gone commando so he could get inside her faster.

He kicked his jeans aside and lifted her up. She wrapped her legs around his waist as he lowered her onto his hard, straining cock. She slid over him, wet and hot, coating him in her slick juices.

"Fuck, baby. I love you."

She gasped.

Unable to take the words back, unwilling to, he drove into her, slamming her back against the wall, taking her harder with the next thrust, burying himself deep inside her until there was nothing separating them but the barrier of clothing. Everything else he'd stripped bare for her.

She shuddered and writhed around him before she cried out, "I'm coming, God, Grey!"

He lost it then. One last thrust and he exploded inside her, giving her everything he had and was, taking her over the edge along with him.

Long after he came down from the high, long after she left, he could only pray she felt the same way.

Grey and Avery took a quick shower together, and she left so she could stop at home, change, and meet her sisters. Grey had planned on spending the day with his music and writing, but Lola had called and wanted to bring lunch by so they could talk. Needing an ear and wanting to clear the air with her, he'd agreed.

When he heard the knock on his door, he opened it, assuming he had to help Lola with packages for lunch. But instead of Lola, he came face-to-face with Simon.

The bastard had somehow talked his way past security, something that would not be happening again.

"What are you doing here?" Grey demanded.

Simon pinned him with his steady gaze. "You've been avoiding my calls."

"I've been busy."

The man pushed past him, letting himself into Grey's apartment without being invited. He pulled off his jacket and draped it over the nearest chair.

"We need to talk. I know Lola's plans. I know my other clients' plans. I don't know yours. And I've had calls from major stars who want you to write for them now that you have time."

Grey folded his arms across his chest, unwilling to let Simon think he ran Grey or his career. "I know."

"Excuse me?"

"I've had the same calls." Grey turned his back on Simon and headed for the kitchen. He opened the fridge and pulled out a bottle of water. He held one out for Simon.

"No thank you," he bit out. "I'm your manager, Grey. You aren't supposed to be talking to anyone unless I'm involved." He pulled on the sleeves of his dress shirt, an agitated tell Grey was used to seeing from the man when he didn't get his way.

And things were about to go downhill.

Grey took a long sip of water and swallowed, gearing up. "Actually you're Tangled Royal's manager. If you gave a shit about what I wanted to do with my career or my life, you'd be my manager too."

Simon stiffened. "What are you saying?"

"You're out, Simon. I appreciate everything you did for me and the band, but you and I don't share the same vision anymore."

Red mottled the man's face. "Ever since you got a bug up your ass about that stupid chick, your priorities have been fucked up. Lola would've continued with the band if you weren't constantly harping on coming home."

Not one part of the man's statement was true. Grey's head throbbed, and the desire to rip Simon's head off for what he'd said about Avery was strong, but so was his sense of self-preservation. A lawsuit was the last thing he needed, and Simon wouldn't hesitate to cause him trouble if he could.

"Get. Out," Grey said, his jaw clenched as hard as his fists at his sides. To emphasize his point, he headed out of the kitchen and into the living area and straight for the front door.

Simon's heavy footsteps followed. He picked up his jacket, his movements jerky, his anger palpable. "You wouldn't be anywhere if it weren't for me, Kingston. And you won't get any-where either."

"My life, my choice," Grey reminded the other man.

"A choice you'll regret," Simon said before storming out, passing Lola on the way.

"Simon?" she called after him.

"Let him go, Lo," Grey said.

Lola stepped inside, and he shut the door behind her. She had bags in her hands, and he grabbed them from her, and they made their way to the kitchen. "What was that all about?" she asked.

"I fired him, and it was a long time coming," he muttered. "If he works for you, that's great, but as far as I'm concerned, he's a pain in the ass. He doesn't care what I want. He blames me for the band breaking up, and worse, he blames Avery. He's rude and insufferable, and I've had enough."

Lola stepped up and hugged him tight. "I get it," she said before easing back.

"He never lost his shit when you got together with Rep. What the hell is his problem?"

"You're his golden boy. Where you go, we go, and he knows it."

Grey shook his head. "You're keeping him around, right?"

Lola met his gaze. "If he can't stand by you or a relationship that makes you happy, then no. I'm through with him too."

Grey blinked, stunned at her statement and loyalty. "You don't need to go that far."

"I do. If he's capable of acting that way with you, who's to say he won't turn on me next? I always told you, even if we're not together professionally, we make a good team. I trust your judgment, Grey. In all things."

His throat grew tight. He was fully aware that this was her way of apologizing for how she'd treated Avery. "She's important to me," he said.

Lola nodded. "I know. And I want you to tell me why. Over dumplings and Chinese food," she said, turning to the bags she'd brought.

Grey grinned as she began to place the containers on his kitchen table, making herself at home. She bounced around his kitchen in her tight leather pants and cropped top, chatting away about Rep's recent hamstring injury. After dealing with pain-in-the-ass Simon, she was a breath of fresh air, and he was glad she'd showed up when she had.

A little while later, his mouth burning from the spicy food, his stomach full, Lola met his gaze across the table.

"I have a question."

He cocked an eyebrow. "Shoot." They'd always been honest with each other, and he wasn't about to stop the flow now.

Lola leaned forward, elbows on the table, empty Chinese food boxes surrounding them. "Why Avery? I mean, let's face it. You had more than your share of women over the years, right? What is it about her that makes you want to give up everything and settle down?"

Grey eyed her, wondering who she was really talking about here. "Is this more about you and Rep than me and Avery?"

"What do you mean?"

He shrugged. "I could ask you the same thing."

She ducked her head, then said, "Okay, fine. I know how I feel about him, but when I think about forever, I wonder how you know. I mean, I do, but I kinda want to hear what you think too."

He nodded. "First, I have to say she's not making me want to give up everything. Or anything. The need to come home, to settle down, quit traveling . . . that's all me. Without Avery, I'd be here. Although I admit, probably not as happily."

Lola laughed. "Okay, that helps to know. I mean, I wouldn't want you to give up a life you loved because the woman in your life couldn't handle it."

Grey rubbed his chest at her mention of Avery not being able to deal. "I'm not going to lie and say I'm not worried about that end of it. I'll always be Grey Kingston from Tangled Royal. If things don't settle around me, I have to hope she can get past her issues."

"One thing at a time. Answer the why, and we'll talk about making it work." Lola began stacking the food boxes, one inside the other.

Grey breathed out hard. "That's the easy thing to answer. From the day we met, she saw *me*. My father saw a disappointment, my mother . . . she had to love me," he said wryly. "It was always tough to make friends because I'd rather be playing my guitar than be with people."

Lola laughed. "I feel that."

"Eventually I met some guys, and we formed a band, but we were a bunch of loners drawn together. We weren't friends. Then I met Avery. I was sitting under a tree with my ever-present notebook. I was struggling with some lyrics I couldn't get right, and she plopped down next to me and offered me one of her cookies."

"The key to a man's heart and all that?" Lola grinned.

Grey groaned at her bad pun. "Hardly. Turns out she was a loner in her own way too. Ever since her father was outed as . . . I don't even know the word for a guy who has two families, but ever since then, she felt alone and ostracized. She got me immediately." He shrugged. He didn't know how to explain their bond. "I never told her I had these huge dreams. Not in so many words. I think she knew I'd go after fame one day. I mean, she did know how much I loved music. She understood it took me out of myself and had always kept me away from the pain at home. But we graduated, and I read an article about an up-and-coming rock star who'd hitchhiked cross-country and made it big. I wanted that."

Lola watched him, understanding clear in her eyes.

Grey grabbed another gulp of water, suddenly parched. "I knew Avery was so bonded to her family she'd never leave, and frankly, selfishly, it never dawned on me to ask her." He ducked his head at the admission. "Once the dream took hold, it wouldn't leave. So I said good-bye one day and was gone the next. I blindsided her."

He'd told Lola a lot over the years, about his family, his life, even about how Avery was his first love. But he'd never told her this. He'd always kept his betrayal deep inside.

She let out a slow whistle. "Okay then. I can understand why Avery is skittish about you. And add her father's life and abandonment into the equation . . ."

"Yeah. But I came home to see if things were still the same for us. If the memory I kept all these years held up over time. And it turns out that, yeah, we still get each other. Still have that deep respect and understanding." The sexual compatibility and chemistry was theirs alone. He didn't need to discuss that with anyone. "I'm not giving up on her," he said.

"I don't think you should." Lola reached across the table and grasped his hand. "And I'll do everything I can to help you make it work."

"Same for you, baby." He grinned at his best friend—next to Avery, of course.

"I know." She winked, then stood up and began cleaning up.

They had each other's backs. Always. And that's why Lola was like family. Now he just had to cement things with Avery in order to make himself and his life complete.

Avery, Olivia, and Sienna agreed to meet at their father's hotel, The Meridian, in South Beach. It wouldn't have been Avery's first choice, but Sienna was on the beach with friends, and it was easiest for her to join them there.

Avery arrived at the restaurant on the water first. Rick left the car with the valet. He stayed close by even though once inside the private hotel, she didn't have to worry about paparazzi. Prying eyes were something else, and she couldn't stop people from looking and recognizing her, but she doubted anyone would.

She settled into a chair facing the ocean and closed her eyes. She breathed in the salty, humid air and tried to relax, but thoughts of hot, sweaty sex with Grey prevented her from mellowing out. He'd taken her against the wall, hard and fast, and she'd let him, giving in without thought, without care. Without a condom.

He'd apologized afterward, sworn he was clean. He had recent blood work to prove it, he'd said, and he hadn't had sex in over six months. She was on the pill, so she wasn't worried about possible pregnancy either. But she hadn't stayed for a long conversation after that, his *I love you* while he was buried deep inside her ringing in the air and inside her head when she'd left. She knew her lack of acknowledging his words had hurt him. Just like she'd hurt him running off this morning.

Except she really had somewhere to be this time. Before she could keep thinking and make herself crazy, Olivia joined her, waddling in, Avery thought with a happy smile. Her sister wore maternity clothes now, and the small bump protruded from the light-blue tank top she wore, along with what looked like black biking shorts, but Avery was sure those, too, were maternity.

"You look so cute!" Avery rose and hugged her sister.

Olivia flushed red. "I feel like a butterball. This kid likes when I eat. I'm always hungry and I'm gaining fast." She patted her stomach.

"Eating for two," Avery said as she settled into her seat.

"At some point, that's not going to be an excuse, right?"

Avery shrugged. "Milk it for all it's worth. When else can you just relax and indulge?"

"That's what Meg said. She seems more relaxed about this whole thing than me." Olivia picked up a glass of ice water and took a long sip.

"Meg is further along and has had more time to get used to the idea of having a baby. Relax. You'll be a natural." Avery knew it was easy for her to reassure her sister when she had no idea what Olivia was going through. She did, however, know that her older sibling would be a wonderful mom.

Before Olivia could respond, Avery caught sight of Sienna and waved. She was twenty-two and the youngest of Robert Dare's children. Like her mother, she had blonde hair, which she'd pulled into a pony tail, and brown eyes. She had a lace cover-up over a bikini, and she joined them, tossing her bag onto an empty chair.

"Hi!" Sienna said, settling into a chair. "Sorry I'm late." Her skin glistened with perspiration from the heat and a healthy tan from the sun.

"You aren't. We haven't even ordered drinks yet," Olivia said, waving to a waiter.

A few minutes later, they'd ordered unsweetened iced teas, and they each chose different salads for lunch, then played catch-up with each other's lives as they ate. After they finished and the plates were cleared away, they sat with refills on their tea and began to discuss the prom event.

Avery pulled a pad from her purse. She already had notes from the meeting at the hospital and the places she and Ella had contacted for help.

"So we have the venue, since the hospital agreed to host there," Avery said. "We can't use flowers, because I don't want to worry about allergies, but I was thinking about using Mylar balloons instead. And what do you think of letting the kids pick the color scheme? We can do a poll or something? Let them be part of things."

"Good idea," Sienna said. "I have a friend who works in party planning. I'm sure she could either get the balloons at a great price or donate them. And I know she has the helium machine. I'll see what she thinks she can do for tablecloths and things."

"Awesome." Avery made a check next to decor.

"Does the hospital have silverware, or do we need to handle that ourselves?" Olivia asked.

Avery responded, and they went back and forth on details, each offering their own ideas.

"What about music?" Sienna finally asked.

Avery bit down on her cheek. "That's the big expense I haven't figured out yet. We can always resort to an iPod and speakers."

"Or my sister, who's dating a rock star, can ask him to sing," Olivia said, then began whistling and looking around innocently.

"Oh my God, yes!" Sienna squealed and practically flew out of her seat at the idea. "I saw the picture of you and Grey Kingston in the paper. That is so cool!"

Avery winced and grabbed her sister's wrist. "Sit and shh." She glanced around to make sure nobody was paying attention.

"Sorry." The younger girl lowered herself into her seat. "But it really is cool."

"Yeah, so cool his stalkers are now my stalkers," Avery muttered under her breath.

"What do you mean?" Olivia asked, leaning across the table.

Avery closed her eyes and sighed, then explained the morning's events and Grey's offer for her to move in with him.

"Crap," Olivia said helpfully.

Avery shot her a look.

"What are you going to do?" Sienna asked.

"I don't know. Ella's away on business, which is good, because I don't want to have to worry about her getting hurt. I also don't want to be alone in my apartment right now, but moving in with Grey? Isn't that . . . I don't know. Extreme?"

"I'd do it in a heartbeat." Sienna shrugged, but Avery knew that was a young mind speaking.

Sienna had missed a year of school thanks to her illness, and she was just going into her senior year of college now. All she was thinking about was Grey Kingston, rock star. She didn't have a clue about the damage Grey could do to Avery's already shaky sense of trust.

"You can always stay with us," Olivia said, reaching out and clasping Avery's hand.

Avery shook her head at Olivia. "Thank you. But I don't want to bring trouble to your door. Same with Mom. Scott and Tyler offered me a place to stay too, but I think I'd kill them both within a day."

Olivia snickered. "Point taken."

"You could take a room here," Sienna suggested.

Avery mulled over that idea, then discarded it. "I think Grey's feelings would be hurt if I chose a hotel over the apartment next door to him."

Olivia pursed her lips and met Avery's gaze.

"What? Just say it," Avery said.

"Fine. You can't move in next door like you're best friends. It's not like he's a one-night stand. You two have history and—"

"He said he loves me." Avery hadn't meant to say the words out loud. She'd been pushing them away ever since hearing them, but they'd kept coming back. Echoing in her head. Pecking away at the shields around her heart.

"Holy shit, that's huge!" Sienna said.

"Not helping," Avery said, shooting her younger sister a grin.

Sienna blushed and shrugged. "Still cool," she said under her breath.

Avery shook her head. "Anyway. You see my issue."

"I see a guy who's got it bad. What's holding you back?" Sienna asked.

"It's complicated, but mostly fear," she admitted. "I don't think he can really know how he'll feel about living here in Miami and giving up the spotlight until he does it. And I don't want to give everything to him only to lose him all over again. So I've been telling myself to live in the moment, and it's worked . . . until now."

"Now that you might have to move in?" Olivia perceptively asked.

Now that she'd realized they weren't just having hot sex, they were making love. She'd panicked and run, but now she had to face those fears to keep herself safe.

"Girls!" a familiar, booming voice said.

Olivia flinched, and Avery stiffened as her father put his hand on the back of her chair.

"Hi, Dad," Sienna said, sounding more subdued. For all her youth, Sienna was a smart, perceptive woman, and she knew exactly what her father's choices had done to his other family.

"Hi," Olivia and Avery said.

He wore a suit as usual, a power play for a man who enjoyed power.

The relationship between his two sets of children had nothing to do with him and everything to do with the bond formed between Sienna and Avery after she'd donated bone marrow. It had started off slowly, but as they'd gotten older, Sienna had kept reaching out, Avery had kept responding, and somehow, the girls had all formed a tight bond. The men? Not as much and not as easily, but Riley and Alex had been best friends, so when she'd ended up with Ian, the men were forced to form a truce. Slowly but surely, everyone had or was coming around.

Ironically, though Robert Dare's blood bound them, his presence caused rifts and old resentments to resurface . . . as evidenced by the sudden headache pulsing behind Avery's eyes. She hadn't heard from her father since her name had been publicly linked with Grey's . . . she couldn't imagine he hadn't heard about the paparazzi swarming her apartment. All her siblings, half and full, were aware. And the man did read the newspaper.

"So what brings you all together?" he asked, still not checking on her well-being. Or Olivia's pregnancy, Avery noted.

Avery didn't believe he was deliberately cruel; he was just selfish and absorbed with his life with Savannah, Sienna's mother, and his family with her.

"We're working on an event that Avery is putting together for children at Miami Children's Hospital. For kids with serious illnesses," Sienna said. "I'm helping out."

He braced a hand on the back of her chair. "Are you sure that's wise? Won't it bring back painful memories?"

At the compassionate tone in her father's voice for his other child, a lump filled Avery's throat. As if sensing her sorrow—or feeling some of it herself—Olivia reached for Avery's hand under the table and squeezed tight. She had her family, the ones who loved her unconditionally, and that's what mattered, she reminded herself. Even if looking into the face of the man who was supposed to lead that family caused her nothing but pain.

"Just the opposite, Dad. I was one of the lucky ones, thanks to Avery," Sienna said, her grateful gaze landing on Avery's.

Avery smiled at the young girl she thought of as a real sister. Sienna's sweet personality and generous nature had to come from somewhere, and more often than not, Avery attributed them to her mom. She hadn't known in the beginning that Robert Dare was married. They became involved, and things got complicated. Avery didn't agree with Savannah's actions, but the blame for everything that had happened lay with Robert Dare.

"Well, I'm proud of you," he said . . . to Sienna. "Have fun, girls," he said, then walked away, his head no doubt already back on business.

Things grew quieter and more strained after his departure, and since they'd covered a lot about the prom already, they agreed to meet again in a week and see what remained for them to line up. Then Avery could take their plans, including a chosen date, back to Dr. McCann for final approval.

The sisters hugged good-bye, and Sienna headed back to the beach to meet up with her friends.

"I'll walk out with you," Olivia said.

"Sounds good," Avery said.

She and her sister strode over to Rick, who was sitting at a neighboring table, discreetly keeping an eye on her.

"All set," she told him.

He rose from his seat and slid a pair of aviators over his eyes. Even Avery had to admit, the man, with his muscles and good looks, was hot.

"Where to?" he asked her.

Avery sighed. Throughout the meal and other conversations, the reality of her situation had never been far from her mind. And after going over and over her options, she knew what she had to do.

"Can you take me home? I need to pack," Avery told Rick.

"Are you going to move in across the hall from Grey?" Olivia asked, her tone clearly conveying she still didn't agree with that choice.

Avery cleared her throat. "No. I'm going to move in *with* him."

Olivia blinked, opening and closing her mouth in surprise.

Avery took advantage of the silence and leaned in to kiss her sister on the cheek. "I'll call you tonight," she said, not wanting to explain herself in front of Rick.

But she didn't blame Olivia for being shocked. Avery had just made the decision herself, after realizing her choices amounted to slim . . . and none. She couldn't stay in her apartment. She wouldn't put a family member in danger, and she couldn't stay at a hotel, not when Grey was offering her two viable alternatives. His extra apartment was nice, but she'd be fooling herself to think she could stay there, with him right next door. There was no reason to. She was already invested in him . . . in them, and she'd be lying to herself to think otherwise.

Chapter Ten

Grey spent an hour at the gym in his building, taking out his frustrations with Simon and life in general on a punching bag. He let himself back into his apartment and immediately stripped off his sweat-slickened shirt and tossed it into the laundry pile in his bedroom. Towel wrapped around his shoulders, he headed for the kitchen, needing a cold drink. At least he felt better, having exerted energy on the inanimate object while pretending it was his ex-manager's face, he thought wryly.

A knock sounded. He wiped his damp head with the towel and opened his door to find Avery standing there, surrounded by suitcases, plural, and Rick, her bodyguard, by her side.

Grey nodded at the other man, acknowledging him, then braced a hand on the doorframe and met Avery's gaze. Before he could speak, the elevator opened behind Rick.

"Call if you need me," the bodyguard said, then stepped back into the waiting car.

Grey looked from her bags, up her long, sexy legs, taking in her cute, flirty dress, before meeting her wide-eyed gaze once more.

"Is this what I think it is?" he asked.

"If you think I'm taking you up on your offer, then yes. It is." She bent down and picked up one of the suitcases. "Help me?" she asked.

"Gladly." She didn't have to ask twice. Except he didn't know where she wanted to stay. "You can keep your stuff in the guest room, where there's more room." He gestured behind him to his apartment. "Unless you want to stay next door?"

She bit down on her lip and shook her head. "No. I want to stay with you."

He hefted the rest of the bags. "Guest room it is," he said, attempting to play it cool and not show his relief at the fact that she didn't want to be an entire hall and apartment and too many locked doors away from him.

He started for the extra bedroom when her voice stopped him. "Grey." He glanced over his shoulder. "You can put my bags in there, but I want to sleep in your bed. With you."

His breath left him in a rush, pleasure and relief soaking into his pores. "Not that I'm not grateful, but what changed since last time I saw you?"

"Let's get rid of the heavy stuff first, okay?"

He nodded and led the way. They unloaded her luggage, freeing their hands. He hadn't been expecting company, and the bedroom was dark, shades drawn.

"Can we talk outside?" she asked.

"Sure." He led her to the terrace, taking her literally outside, whether she'd meant it or not.

Though it was humid, it was nice to be outdoors. As always, the fresh air and the view of the city reminded him of how lucky he was to live here. And when Avery settled against one of the oversized loungers, looked up at him, and smiled, he knew his luck was holding.

He sat on the edge of her lounge and waited for her to talk, sensing she had a lot on her mind. She glanced up at the sky, her eyes narrowing, her cute nose wrinkled against the glare of the sun. Light freckles dotted the bridge, and he had the sudden desire to taste each one.

"I saw my father today," she said.

Her words brought him down from the beginning of a light, fun fantasy.

"On purpose?" he asked. Because she hadn't mentioned seeing the parent she had a difficult relationship with as being part of her day.

She shook her head. "You know Olivia, Sienna, and I had lunch at The Meridian. It wouldn't have been my first choice, but Sienna was already there at the beach with her friends. Like I told you, we were planning for the hospital prom, and my father walked over."

She hesitated, and Grey gave her all the time she needed to gather her thoughts.

"I haven't heard from my dad at all. Not when our picture was in the paper." She gestured between them. "Not after the paparazzi swarmed my apartment or when some crazy person left a message on my door. And the family is big enough that someone had to have told him." She raised her shoulder in a nonchalant shrug he wasn't buying for one second. "He must have heard about it . . . and dismissed it from his mind."

Shit, Grey thought, his heart clenching at the hurt she tried so hard to pretend didn't exist. Her old man had no idea the emotional damage he'd caused all of his kids, but because Avery had been the donor to his other child, her emotions had been hit most directly.

As someone who'd been belittled by a parent, Grey understood that *no comment* could be as painful as a negative one. Both kinds of behavior left a kid feeling unworthy and unimportant, two things he never ever wanted Avery to feel. But he had caused her to experience that feeling of abandonment as well, and he was coming to realize putting it behind her wasn't as simple as he'd naïvely hoped it would be.

She would never understand how much he regretted suddenly disappearing from her life all those years ago, how much he hated himself for doing it. He could have kept in touch, let her know she'd always been important to him, that out of sight wasn't out of mind. He hadn't. But the fact remained, he was here now, and he intended to make up for every last slight and hurt she'd ever felt.

"What did your father say today?" Grey asked, holding his breath for her answer.

Avery twisted her fingers together until the tips turned white. "He told Sienna he was proud of her for getting involved with kids with cancer after all she'd been through."

"He's an asshole," Grey stated. He pushed himself up and straddled the chair until he sat closer to where she was curled into herself.

He grasped her hands, easing her grip and massaging the blood flow back into her fingers, holding onto her now, when she needed him most.

"I try and tell myself I don't care, that I don't need him, that it doesn't matter whether or not he sees or acknowledges me." Avery met his gaze, and tears leaked from her violet eyes. "But it does."

"Of course it does," he agreed. "Just like it matters to me that I never got my father's approval. It matters that I know that, even if he'd lived, I still wouldn't get approval or encouragement today. Doesn't matter how successful I am."

"Your father was crazy," she whispered. "You're an amazing man, Grey. It doesn't matter if he saw it or not, knew it or not."

"Exactly." He grinned because she'd played into his hands, made his point for him. "Same applies to you, sugar. You're an amazing woman. And you were a brave kid, giving bone marrow to your sister."

She shook her head. "I didn't really understand the magnitude of what they asked me to do. I just did what my parents wanted." She drew a deep breath and looked down at their intertwined hands as she spoke. "And a part of me did it for selfish reasons, so my father would finally see me as something special."

She spoke so softly he had to strain to hear her.

"I prayed that he would be so happy and grateful that I'd saved his other daughter, he'd come back home." Avery bowed her head, her long hair falling over her face at the admission.

God, he hurt for her. "You were a kid. All those feelings, they were *normal.* You were just wishing and hoping for things every child should have. It doesn't change the fact that you were brave then and you were strong afterward. Like you told me the other day, your entire life shifted because of what your father did. The press coming after you, the panic attacks, the anxiety. You dealt with it all. Without him there to support you."

Avery raised her head and met Grey's understanding gaze. "You really believe that?" she asked.

"I do." He squeezed her hands in reassurance.

Avery allowed his words and his belief in her to settle inside her. To warm her up where she'd always been cold. Because what she'd just admitted to him now? She'd never told anyone before, not even the therapist that her mother had sent her to.

Yes, she'd given bone marrow. But she'd always believed that her motives made her selfish. And though as an adult, she donated her time to sick kids at the hospital and enjoyed seeing them light up and feel better about themselves, a part of her was trying to atone and make up for those selfish thoughts and needs she'd had as a kid.

But here was Grey, telling her that those old childhood feelings had been valid. For the first time, she pushed aside the juvenile view she'd tortured herself with for years and looked at things as an adult. As Grey did. And the heaviness that was always in her chest when she thought of that time, of her father or Sienna, lifted a little.

"Thank you," Avery said.

"It's just the truth, sugar." He grinned, and she melted inside, the heat of the afternoon sun having nothing on the heat Grey generated inside her.

Because she was finally looking at him, and she was instantly aware of more than her own emotions. His tanned, bare chest filled her line of vision, and her pulse began a heavy beat in her veins. Desire kicked in, making itself known in telling ways, her sex filling with need, her breasts suddenly heavy and aching to be touched.

"Now let's get back to what changed your mind about staying here, with me," he said.

"Oh, that."

He cocked an eyebrow. "Yeah, that."

She blew out a deep breath, forcing herself to concentrate on what he needed for a change, and that was answers.

They weren't simple, but she owed him the truth. "On the one hand, there's the practical consideration. I really do need to stay someplace safe."

He nodded. "We all agree on that. But if safe is all you're looking for, across the hall works just fine."

He was right. "I know. But after everything that happened with my father at lunch, all I wanted to do was see you. I wanted to talk to you." Her mind had been filled with thoughts of him. "I already knew I had to make a decision about where to go, and after talking to my sisters, I realized I'd be deluding myself if I thought I could stay anywhere but *with* you." She drew a deep breath for courage and said, "We click, Grey. And I can't run from that anymore."

"Thank fuck," he muttered, and she couldn't help but grin.

"I can't promise what the future will bring," she had to add. "But I'm here now, and I'm trying to give this thing a shot."

It wasn't something she'd consciously decided at lunch; rather, as she'd sat here unloading her burdens, letting him help her ease her pain, she'd understood running away was no longer an option. She needed to try.

At Avery's words, Grey's heart pounded hard in his chest. She was baring her soul in a way she'd never done before, because it pertained to them. She was admitting that she was as invested as he was . . . he hoped. But he also knew his own needs could be setting him up for a hard fall he wasn't prepared to take. He heard what she was saying, but he had to make sure he processed correctly.

"We need to be clear, sugar. I want to see where things go *for real.* Are you on board?"

Her honest, open gaze met his. "I am."

She'd just given him everything he'd asked for and all he needed to hear. He pulled her across his lap and managed to twist so she straddled him now. The skirt from her dress flipped up easily on its own, her moist panties coming into direct heated contact with his rigid cock, which strained against his workout shorts.

"Mmm. You feel good." She rocked her hips and, at the same time, placed her hands on his bare chest, skimming his flesh with her orange-painted fingernails.

Goose bumps and arousal hit him hard.

"You feel better." He slid her dress up and over her head, tossing it to the ground at their feet.

"We're outside," she said, her eyes open wide.

"We are." He flicked his wrist and divested her of her bra, adding to the pile, then cupped her breasts in his hands, squeezing the mounds with his palms before zeroing in on her pert nipples, tweaking and toying with each.

"Oh God." She rolled her hips against his dick, moaning as she obviously hit the right spot.

He gritted his teeth, counting in his head, holding back the need pulsing through him at breakneck speed. If he let go, he'd come hard in his pants like a teenager with no control. And that wasn't happening.

"I want to see you come for me. Right here under the warm sun and open air." His apartment was high enough that nobody else could see her. Nobody could share in the bounty that was Avery.

"I need to," she said in a hoarse voice, her nipples tight, body trembling.

He leaned in and pulled one of her nipples into his mouth, swirling his tongue around the distended tip before grazing the hard nub with his teeth.

She whimpered and arched her back, pushing her breast deeper. He plucked at her other one before switching it up, wrapping his lips around the other nipple and playing with the damp one with his fingers. All the while, she moaned and sighed, rocking against him and keeping him riding the edge.

Unable to wait, he slid his free hand into the waistband of her barely there panties and cupped her wet heat. "Fuck, sugar, you're soaking."

"Just for you." She rolled her hips back and forth, her sighs louder, music to his very attuned ears.

"Come for me now, and I'll make sure it's the first of many." He felt confident making that promise, since his cock pulsed in rhythm to her now-jerky moves, ready for action.

He slid his finger over her clit, rubbing back and forth, until she gripped his head, pulled at his hair, and screamed her climax as her body shuddered around his hand and over his confined dick. He kept the pressure on her sex until she collapsed against him.

"That was beautiful," he said, bracing his hands around her cheeks and pressing a kiss to her lips. "You ready for more?"

Her heavy eyelids lifted, and she met his gaze. "Bring it on."

He chuckled, liking this brave, open Avery. He lifted her up and moved her to the edge of the lounge. He slid his shorts off and kicked them aside, then reached for her panties and removed them with one quick pull.

"Grey!"

"No time for subtle seduction. I'm ready to come, and it's got to be inside you."

His normally more reserved Avery scooted back in the chair and spread her legs wide. Her shaved, pink pussy glistened and beckoned to him, which was clearly her intent. He met her open gaze, and he knew what a gift she was giving him. That she was willing to try a relationship, to put her insecurities aside—that was everything.

He moved over her. Her gaze dropped to where his cock poised at her entrance, her juices coating his head before he even slid inside. He'd never forget the sight, wanted her to take it in too.

But he also wanted her attention when he thrust home, inside the only place he belonged. "Look at me," he said, barely recognizing his desire-roughened tone.

Her violet eyes met his as he inched into her body, slowly filling her up as completely as she did his heart. In her gaze, he saw acceptance of them, and everything he hoped for.

No longer could he hold back. One fast jerk of his hips and he joined them completely, and not just where their bodies connected. Her breasts slid against his chest, her nipples rasping against him. She wrapped her arms around his back, and he felt the beat of her heart, pounding solidly against his chest. He no longer needed to look into her eyes to know they were bound in every possible way. He wasn't letting her go and prayed outside forces wouldn't work against them or rip them apart.

Then he stopped thinking, because his hips shifted and he saw stars. He moved, rubbing against her clit, and she gasped at the sensation.

"I promised you more, remember?" he asked, not letting up on the pressure until he rocked her into another orgasm, her moans and sighs bringing him almost to the edge.

Once the quakes of her body subsided, he pulled out. His cock was aching and hard, but he wanted one more climax out of her. Wanted to take her places nobody else ever had or would again.

"What are you doing?" she asked, almost limp beneath him.

"Want you on top." He eased her up, slid beneath her, and settled her astride him, his rigid erection easily sliding back into her.

"I can't. Not again," she said, but her actions belied her words, and she began to ride him, her body taking over any purported exhaustion.

"Oh God!" Her eyes opened wide as he obviously hit her sweet spot, and damned if he didn't light up from within too.

"Harder, Grey!"

Fuck. His entire body was already rigid, his balls drawing up tight. He was so damn close already. His hips involuntarily jerked up, and she screamed.

"Oh shit, I'm coming again," she cried, her words a moan as she bucked against him, sucking his cock in deep, her slick walls contracting around him. "Grey!"

He let go then, his climax lost in the sexy, beautiful sounds of her release. He spilled everything he had and everything he was inside her, until she collapsed, her limp body draping over his.

A week into their new status quo, Avery couldn't believe how seamlessly her life meshed with Grey's. She liked the right side of the bed, he already slept on the left. She was a grump without coffee in the morning, he owned a machine with a timer that he was used to presetting the night before. And in realizing he had a huge sexual appetite, she discovered an untapped part of herself that felt the same way.

In past relationships, she didn't normally spend the night or let a guy stay over. She wasn't a cuddler, and she didn't like awkward mornings after. And since she hadn't been all that into sex with the bland guys she'd deliberately chosen after Grey, wrapping it up quickly had been easy. She knew, thanks to her previous times with Grey, that he'd exceeded every experience she'd ever had . . . or would ever have. What she didn't know was that once they lived together, she would come to crave him so badly.

Morning sex? A necessity. Before bed? Hell yes. More than once, if he had any say. Cuddling became mandatory. Quickies during the day? Check and check. In fact, with Grey being a work-from-home guy and her a work-from-home girl, she was pretty sure she'd turn into a nymphomaniac if they kept things up.

Sex aside, their days meshed too. In the early morning, he exercised at the gym in his condo, and Avery worked on either a written blog or video. One day during the week, Rick drove her to the hospital to volunteer with the kids.

As far as the taping, she didn't want her viewers to know anything was different, so Grey went to her place and picked up the poster that was always her backdrop for her video blogs and hung it up on an empty wall in the guest room. Earlier in the week, Olivia had come over and helped her set up the guest room so she could do videos surrounded by her makeup and accessories. Somehow, she was able to make it work. In the afternoons, Avery made them lunch like she would do for herself at home, and dinners were a mix of ordering in, one of them cooking, or going out.

The paparazzi, after circling her at the apartment, had seemingly disappeared. No more mentions on blogs or newspapers, and Grey had his legal counsel on notice just in case something happened again. Granted, it had only been a few days, but Avery appreciated the lack of attention, not just on her but on them. They were able to focus on themselves, and while they were wary and careful, there were no huge incidents to hit Avery's anxiety or cause her concern for the future.

He liked to work on his music or meet with the contractor for the apartment next door in the afternoons, and that's when Avery dragged Rick around town to get sponsors for the prom she had planned. Life went on, and work didn't suffer.

And when she and Grey wanted to go out for a meal, they would duck out of his parking garage, alternating between her BMW and Rick's unobtrusive black sedan, so they could go somewhere for lunch or dinner unnoticed. They drove an hour beyond Miami and found fun places where they could walk the beach and be alone. She wondered if it was possible that, with time, the curiosity about Grey and the other band members would disappear completely. While reminding herself that a week hardly set a precedent, she'd begun to feel more than a sliver of hope.

Hope was a dangerous thing, but she couldn't contain hers, not when she was experiencing a level of happiness as an adult that she'd always thought was beyond her. And she wanted to hold onto it for all she was worth.

A few days later, Lola called early one morning, asking Avery if she'd like to meet for lunch. Avery had woken up with a migraine headache and wasn't up to driving, but she was curious about what Lola wanted, so she had invited her over instead.

She hadn't seen the other woman since the awkward night at Lola and Rep's house, and Grey hadn't mentioned her. He was at a meeting with Chloe Mandrake, lead singer of the punk rock band Night Madness, about Grey writing a song and collaborating with them for their next album.

When Avery had asked him about whether or not he needed a manager, he'd said he'd rather use his lawyer to deal with contracts if things reached that point. Meanwhile, he seemed excited about the opportunity, and to her surprise, Avery was too. She didn't want to hold him back in his career, and she didn't want him to feel like he couldn't move forward because of her anxiety or fears. She wanted to believe in them, and she was *trying* as promised.

Which didn't mean she wasn't intimidated by the fact Grey was hanging out with the punk rock princess, who was definitely sexy and hot with her tattoos, heavy makeup, and curvy body. She was. And she knew Chloe lived in LA, and she'd be foolish not to think Grey would need to travel sometimes in order to work with her and the band. But he came home to her at night. And she was *trying*.

Lola arrived, dressed in a short, short miniskirt, bright-red ankle-high cowboy-style boots, and a crop top over a bandeau. And Avery reminded herself once again, Grey came home to *her*. And she was trying.

"I really appreciate you letting me come over," the other woman said.

"I was surprised to hear from you."

Lola took a seat across from Avery on the outside patio. Good thing she was in a single chair, surrounded by white wrought-iron tables, and not on the lounger where Avery and Grey had consummated their new relationship agreement. Avery chose that seat for herself.

Avery pulled a pillow over her lap and tucked one knee beneath her, attempting unsuccessfully not to think about *that* day with Grey. She flushed with heat at the memory of how she'd been naked on the terrace, her boobs and ass out for the world to see. Not the world, since nobody had a view here, but it had sure felt that way. She hadn't cared.

After the way her father had ignored all that was important in Avery's life and even Avery herself that day, all she'd wanted was Grey. Because he looked at her like she mattered. He touched her like she was his reason for being, and she knew if she dropped her walls, she'd admit she felt the same way.

She'd needed him then, wanting everything Grey had to offer her too much to worry about propriety or being naked outdoors.

"Avery? Are you okay? Your cheeks are red," Lola said, bringing her out of her fantasies.

"Just the headache," she murmured, although in reality, the headache was almost gone.

"Do you want to sit inside where it's cooler?" Lola offered.

"Maybe in a little while. I'm okay for now, thanks."

Lola nodded. "So I guess you're wondering why I called?"

Avery managed a nod despite the mild pounding in her head.

"To apologize. I would have called you sooner, but I know you had a lot going on with the paps and the other issues. I just . . . I was looking out for a friend, and I did it the wrong way." To the other woman's credit, she looked genuinely contrite. And from what Avery knew of Grey, he wouldn't pick a best friend who wasn't a good person.

"I have older brothers who can't manage to butt out of my life. And a sister who would do the same given the opportunity, so I get it. You're his family, and I want you to know I respect that."

Lola blinked, and Avery wondered if she was choked up. "You have no idea how relieved I am," Lola said, her voice cracking, confirming Avery's suspicions.

Avery leaned forward and met the other woman's gaze. "I won't hurt him without breaking my own heart in the process.

I know that's not everything you want to hear, but it's the best I can do."

"Nobody's perfect, especially me." Lola met her gaze, and Avery believed an understanding had been reached. "So how is the prom planning going? Grey told me all about it."

Avery smiled, pleased Lola was asking about her pet project. She'd been on the phone all week and had met with so many different people, changing up the basic idea. She was excited to share it with Lola.

"It's great. We decided to copy the model at Memorial Sloan Kettering Children's Hospital in New York. Instead of teenagers only, we're doing a party for all the kids in the cancer wing of the hospital. It's a combination pediatric and teen prom, so everyone has something to look forward to."

Lola smiled. "That's so amazing. I really admire your dedication."

"I . . ." Avery cleared her throat and decided to just say why she'd researched other hospitals and changed her plans. "I donated bone marrow to my half sister when I was nine. I know what it would have meant to her to have something fun on the horizon. Young or old, girls love to dress up, right? And the boys . . . well, they'll deal."

"I love the idea. I really do. And so will the kids."

"I hope so, because I had to call shops all over Miami who cater to all different ages, boys and girls, to get dresses and clothes. It's been a huge undertaking, but I'm thrilled. The hospital finally gave the official okay yesterday." She'd met with Dr. McCann, and he'd been so impressed with the amount of sponsorships he'd agreed on the spot.

"Anything I can do to help?" Lola asked.

Avery would never impose on one of Grey's friends for an in-person appearance, but since Lola was asking . . . "Would you mind signing pictures or something for the kids? We could put them in the goodie-slash-giveaway bags for the end of the night."

Lola's expression lit up at the idea. "I'd love to. Let me see what I can get my hands on. Text me the date, and I'll make sure you have things in time."

Avery clapped her hands in excitement, just imagining the kids' expressions to have something signed by Lola Corbin.

They chatted for a little while longer before Lola rose to her feet. "I'm going to let you rest now, but thanks for seeing me. And for accepting my apology."

Avery waved away her words. "It's in the past."

"Good. I hope we can try dinner, the four of us, again?"

"I'd like that."

Avery walked Lola back into the apartment just as Grey stepped inside. From the expression on his face, either his meeting hadn't gone well . . . or something else was very wrong.

Chapter Eleven

Grey should have known Simon wouldn't go away quietly. But he'd been sidetracked by how good things had been. With the paparazzi focused on the breakup of a Hollywood super couple, they'd left Tangled Royal, Grey Kingston, and his old flame alone. Whoever had broken into Avery's apartment building and vandalized her front door had disappeared. He and Avery were getting to know each other again, and things were almost perfect. Which meant he should have known to watch his back.

Grey's meeting with Chloe Mandrake hadn't gone as expected. Not in any imaginable way. And though he knew he should have cooled off before heading home, he also knew he could only take out his anger in the gym, on a punching bag. He hadn't expected to find Lola here with Avery, but considering this had to do with his ex-manager, Lola needed the information to make her own decisions on what to do with the man.

"What's wrong?" Avery asked the second she saw him. Yeah, she read him well, and he was grateful for it.

"I can go," Lola offered.

Grey shook his head. "You need to hear this."

"What is it?" Lola asked.

Avery watched him with a concerned expression.

He blew out a sharp breath. "I just met with Chloe Mandrake. She'd already contacted me about collaborating on a song for her next album, based on the work I did with Alden Mills."

"That's really cool!" Lola said, her eyes lighting up. "You two would rock it."

"Not jealous?" Grey asked, grateful for the moment to put aside his fury. He playfully nudged her with his elbow, and she grinned.

"No. I know I'm your true band sister."

Avery laughed. "None of this explains what has you so upset."

"Chloe said she didn't know if she could go forward with the collaboration. She said the reason she wanted to do it in the first place was because I cowrote with Alden Mills." He shoved his hands into his slacks pockets. "But Simon told her that wasn't the truth. That Mills did the writing and took me along just to take advantage of my popularity and audience." Grey's stomach was still twisted into angry knots over the accusation.

"That bastard," Lola said, digging through her bag and pulling out her phone.

"What are you doing?" Grey asked.

"Calling him and giving him a piece of my mind!"

"Slow down!" Grey reached for the phone and placed it on the table.

Lola huffed at him. "You expect me to do nothing?"

"I expect you to let me handle it."

"Did Chloe believe him?" Avery asked.

He shrugged. "She wants to believe me, but she's on a tight deadline, and working with me if I can't hack it is a risk."

Avery came up beside him and wrapped an arm around his waist in an obvious attempt to calm him. He tucked her into him, grateful for her support and for Lola's, even if she was, as usual, impulsive in her defense.

"What are you going to do?" Lola asked.

"Mills's widow is the only one who was there during our sessions. Other than Simon," he muttered. "She's well aware of what Alden was and wasn't capable of when we worked together. I called the last number I had for Mills, and it's been disconnected."

Lola swore.

He glanced at Avery. "I called your brother on the way home and hired his firm to find Mills's widow."

"I hope he didn't give you a hassle first."

"No. He takes work and security seriously," Grey assured her. And he had. For all the shit Tyler gave him over Avery, he was damned good at his job and didn't joke around. "And I left a message for my lawyer. I want to find out what constitutes slander, because I'm not letting Simon get away with this bullshit."

Avery squeezed him tighter, and he drew strength from knowing she had his back and wasn't running.

Lola groaned. "Well, whatever you need, I'm here. And you can bet I'm firing his ass too."

Grey held up one hand. "Not yet. I don't want to piss him off even more. I let him go and he retaliated. Let me see what my options are first. Just don't sign anything new with him."

Lola narrowed her gaze, her pout strong, but she nodded in agreement. "Don't worry. I won't." She snatched her phone. "Call me if you need me." She strode out the door, shutting it behind her.

Once they were alone, Avery pulled out of his arms and met his gaze. "I can't believe Simon would undermine you like that. After all those years together?"

"He was always a slimy bastard, but he was our slimy bastard." He paused, then said, "Do I want to know what you and Lola were doing here together?" he asked.

"She apologized in person for her behavior when we met. She was really being nice. She's donating signed goodies for the hospital prom. Don't worry about me and Lola. You have enough stress right now. And speaking of stress . . . why don't you come into the bedroom and let me work on your tension," she said, her voice getting husky.

Before he could process her tone or intent, she stepped in front of him and reached for the button on his pants. He'd dressed up for this meeting, wanting to make a good impression on Chloe, punk rocker or not, and the pants slid easily to the floor.

Avery pulled his boxer briefs down, her nails raking down his thighs as she dropped to her knees in front of him. "Holy hell," he muttered.

She wrapped her fingers around his thick cock, and her tongue darted out as she took a small, tentative lick. The combination of her warm breath, soft tongue, and the fact that this was his Avery had heat and arousal spiraling through him.

He locked his knees to remain upright and glanced into her face. A sexy smile teased her lips before she opened her mouth and took him inside.

Avery was no expert, but she wanted to give back to Grey. He'd done nothing but be good to her, try to convince her how good they could be together, and she was finally starting to believe. To relax enough to stop thinking about herself and want to take care of him for a change.

She braced one hand on his thigh, wrapped the other around his shaft, and pulled him in deep. She swirled her tongue over him while pumping her hand back and forth, judging her success by the low rumbles coming from his chest.

To her surprise, the sounds of his pleasure aroused her on a whole different level than she'd ever experienced before. It was a heady experience, being in charge, and her body responded in kind. Her breasts hurt in the best possible way, and her sex swelled, feeling empty and needy.

He began to thrust gently, keeping a hand on top of her head, trying not to hurt her while he moved in time to the workings of her tongue, her lips, and even, lightly, her teeth.

She squeezed her thighs together, enjoying the rush of arousal she got while taking him higher.

Suddenly he pulled on her hair. "Gonna come, sugar."

She knew he was giving her a warning, telling her to let him go, but she wanted this. Wanted his release and surrender. All his alert did was make her concentrate more, on the glide of her hand over his cock and the working of her mouth, drawing him in and taking him as deep as she could go.

He came with a roar of satisfaction, and she swallowed every drop, pulling out only after he'd spent himself completely.

He yanked her to her feet and kissed her forehead before unexpectedly lifting her into his arms. "That was awesome," he told her, dropping her on the bed and yanking her shorts off, taking her panties with them.

"Grey!"

His eyes darkened as he gazed down at her swollen sex. "Your turn," he said gruffly. He dipped his head and dragged his tongue along her damp slit.

She moaned at the contact, her skin sensitive and aroused already. He teased her with wicked nips of his teeth, soothed with sweet laps of his tongue, and finally slid one long finger inside her. She moaned and bent her knees, trying to contract around him and pull him deeper.

He raised his head and blew over her damp pussy.

The warmth of his breath whipped her into even more of a frenzy of need, and she curled her fingers into the bedding.

"I've got you," he said, his words a drugging promise.

"Please, please." She needed to come and wasn't ashamed to beg for it.

He curled his finger inside her, pressing against the spot only he'd ever found.

She moaned as her body began to shake and contract, her orgasm exploding without warning, taking her up and over. Sparkles flickered behind her eyes; warmth and sensation took her body over. By the time she came back to earth, Grey was propped on an elbow, his gorgeous face staring into hers.

"You're fucking gorgeous when you climax. But you're even more beautiful when you make me come."

A hot flush stained her cheeks, and she couldn't find the words to respond.

"I'm definitely more relaxed now," he said, speaking when she didn't.

"Good." She closed her eyes and realized her headache was gone. Maybe she'd found a cure, she thought, unable to hold back a laugh.

"What's so funny?"

"I think orgasms are the cure for migraines," she said, still giggling.

He grinned. "Happy to oblige any time."

She ran a hand through his mussed hair. "So what are you going to do about the problem with Simon?" she asked, hesitant to bring up the situation but knowing there was no way he'd put it out of his head completely.

He blew out a long breath. "Refrain from killing him and wait to hear from your brother. I need to prove I wrote those lyrics, and only Mills's widow can verify my claim."

As if on cue, his cell rang, a muted sound from his pants in the other room. He shot her a regretful look and rose from the bed. She couldn't help but stare at his gorgeous, tight ass as he headed into the den for his phone.

Too soon he disappeared from sight. He returned, talking as he walked in and stood beside the bed.

This time her gaze fell to his strong thighs and the semi-hard erection. He glared at her as he spoke, a silent warning to stop distracting him. She grinned and rose from the bed, looking for her shorts.

"So that's it? She's out of the country with no forwarding information?" he asked, his frustration clear.

She pulled on her panties and shorts, snapping them.

"Yes. I know you're still looking. Thanks and keep me posted." Grey hit end and tossed his phone onto the bed.

"Dead end?" she asked.

"For now. Tyler said they're still trying to find her. Neighbors and friends said she went into seclusion after her husband's death."

"But she has to surface some time. Mail, bills, things still need attending to," Avery said. "Have faith in Tyler and whoever he put on her trail."

"I will." He'd retrieved a pair of sweats from a drawer and pulled them on, covering up Avery's favorite view before turning toward her. "I'm sorry for why you're here," he said. "But I'm damned glad you are."

"Me too," she murmured and was surprised to realize she meant it, her fears and objections fading with each passing day.

A few days later, Tyler called Grey and asked to see him at the office regarding his investigation into Mills's widow. Grey was pumped that Tyler had information already.

Avery would have loved to go along, but she'd had a meeting scheduled with Dr. McCann at the hospital, and afterward, she'd promised Ella, who was returning from her trip, that she would pick her up from the airport, so Grey headed over alone.

No sooner had he walked into the man's office than he was ambushed. Both Tyler and Scott Dare awaited him, and though he wanted to believe it was because they were co-owners of Double Down Security, he braced himself for them to gang up on him about leaving Avery. Which wouldn't be fucking happening.

"Gentlemen," he said as politely as he could manage, his hands in tight fists, his muscles strained.

"Have you seen the morning paper?" Tyler asked without preamble.

"Online or print," Scott added. "Either one will do."

Neither man seemed pleased, and Grey grew even more agitated. "No."

Tyler walked around to the big screen on his desk and turned it to face him. "Someone's playing dirty."

Grey skimmed a variety of headlines that had been pulled up on all the gossip sites and online newspapers with Grey's name jumping out from them.

Tyler zeroed in on one article and pulled it up for reading. Grey stalked over. Bracing his arms on the desk, he leaned down and skimmed long enough to get the gist. Allegations and speculation that Grey Kingston hadn't written or even cowritten songs on his famous collaboration with Alden Mills. *And if he hadn't written those, what had he really contributed to Tangled Royal?*

Grey saw red. If Simon were in front of him, he'd take a swing first, no questions asked.

"Breathe out," Scott told him.

Grey listened, pulling in much-needed air. "Is that why you called me over? To show me my manager's effectively killing any kind of writing career before it starts?"

"No, we're calling you to tell you we found the widow," Scott said.

"This is icing," Tyler muttered, pointing to the computer.

"Shut up," Scott muttered to his brother before turning his eerily Avery-like eyes on Grey. "As far as I'm concerned, jury's out on you until you prove yourself with my sister. This jackass over here"—he gestured to his brother—"he doesn't know what it's like to be in love. You *are* in love with her, right?"

Leave it to a Dare brother to put his cards on the table. "Yes, I love her."

"Hearts, flowers, who gives a shit? The fact is—" Tyler began.

"My relationship with Avery is my business, not yours," Grey said. "I've already told you you can trust me with your sister's welfare, and you can. The rest is not up for discussion unless it involves keeping her safe."

Scott eyed him with respect. Tyler ignored him.

Grey could live with that. "I hired you to do a job because I have to shut Simon down," Grey said. "What did you find out about Mills's widow?"

"Dawn Mills is in seclusion in the mountains. To contact her, you have to leave a message at the town store. They wait for her to come down and give her messages. Then it's up to her whether or not she returns them."

"Sounds great," he said sarcastically.

"Yeah, but we started that process on your behalf," Tyler said.

Grey nodded. When it came to the professional, he knew he could count on the man. "Good. Keep me posted. Is that all?"

"No," Tyler said. "The longer my sister lives with you, the more chance she'll end up emotionally invested and hurt."

Grey shook his head. "You're so determined not to trust me. I think it's time you took a harder look at yourself than me." Grey stuck his hand out for Scott.

The other man shook it.

He merely nodded at Tyler. "You need me, you know where to find me."

He needed to get home so he'd be there when Avery returned. Because she was what mattered in his life right now.

With her ever-present bodyguard, Rick, by her side, Avery picked up Ella from the airport. Rick drove her car, and Avery chatted with him from the passenger seat. When she got past his business personality, she liked the man. But he always kept an eye out for danger, which she appreciated. Not that she anticipated any issues. Simon causing Grey trouble seemed to be the main thing going on at the moment. Avery was no longer the flavor of the month, for which she was grateful.

She'd had time to think and realized that as scary as some of the moments had been, she'd survived them quite well as an adult. She was proud of herself. Happy she could be with Grey and give this thing a real chance.

Avery and Rick waited for Ella at baggage claim. While she'd been away for work, Avery had explained what had happened with one of Grey's groupies or a stalker getting as close as their front door. And she'd told her friend that she was temporarily living with Grey. She'd also informed Ella that Tyler had declared their shared apartment off-limits to single women living alone. Because Tyler had set down the mandate, Ella had immediately disagreed. She didn't want to disrupt her life at Tyler's demand.

Grey had grabbed the phone from Avery and offered Ella the use of his extra condo across the hall because he didn't think it was safe for her to be there if someone came looking for Grey or Avery and found Ella there instead.

Avery wanted to kiss her sweet man. She couldn't believe he was willing to put off his studio renovation, but he swore he didn't mind. Avery liked knowing not only was Ella safe, but she was across the hall, and her friend had given in.

Ella walked into the arrival area, looking tan from her island trip and the photo shoots outdoors. Floppy-brimmed hat in hand, she pulled Avery into a hug. "I am so glad to be back!"

"Glad to have you back."

"We have a lot of catching up to do," she said, eyeing the tall, broad, imposing-looking bodyguard by Avery's side.

Avery grinned. "We do, but not now." She wasn't going to discuss her love life and especially not her sex life in front of Rick. "I have many other things to tell you. I met with Dr. McCann this morning." She patted her bag, her calendar secure inside. "We have dates for the kids to choose their dresses and another for the fittings so we don't wear the kids out."

Ella nodded. "I can't wait to go visit them. It's been a while, and I want to see their faces in person. See how they're doing."

Avery nudged her side. "I'm sure they'll love to hear about your adventures on the island."

Ella grinned. "I brought back fun gifts for them too."

"That's so sweet." But no surprise to Avery. Ella was a good person. "And don't forget, I have to give you the dates for everything. I need you there."

Avery met Ella's gaze. She'd hated booking things without her friend there, but Dr. McCann was leaving on vacation tomorrow. It had to be done today.

Ella waved a tanned hand through the air. "I'll make it work. My boss is flying high after this successful assignment. It'll be fine."

They walked to the carousel and waited for Ella's luggage. "Your bodyguard is hot," Ella whispered.

"Are you interested?" Avery asked, thrilled her friend seemed to be actively looking at a man, not keeping her feelings hidden as usual.

"No," Ella said too quickly.

Avery blew out a frustrated breath. She was tired of the evasion and lies. "Who is he?" Avery asked her friend. "Who's got you tied up in knots, and why are you hiding things from me?"

Ella grasped Avery's shoulders and met her gaze. "Maybe one day I'll be able to talk about it," she said. She looked over her shoulders and scanned the metal carousel. "Oh, look! My duffel." She pointed to a black bag with a huge pink bow.

A lucky diversion this time.

Rick rolled his eyes at the huge decoration that marked the bag before plucking the luggage off and gesturing for the women to walk beside him. They followed him toward the car, and both did their best not to laugh as the big, strong man wheeled the bag with the tacky pink ribbon on the handle, mumbling about the indignities of the job as he walked and kept an eye on everything around them at all times.

The next stop was their apartment, so Ella could pack clothes for moving into Grey's. On the ride, Ella went on about her trip to Turks and Caicos and the photo shoot, the crazy photographer, and the models. Avery loved her stories, and even Rick seemed mildly amused.

Until they pulled into the parking lot and exited the car, only to run into Avery and Ella's neighbors.

"Hi, Gary," Ella said.

Avery smiled at the man.

Rick tried to keep them moving indoors, but Gary liked to talk. He always had. He was prematurely bald—not bad-looking, just not Avery's type. He was in his thirties and lived with his girlfriend in the apartment next door, and they'd always been nice, good neighbors.

"I'm sorry to hear the papers are dredging up the past," he said, looking at Avery.

"What?"

Even Rick tuned in now, stepping in closer.

"What do you mean?" Ella asked.

Gary's cheeks burned red. "I'm sorry. I thought you knew."

Avery believed him. Gary wasn't a gossip. He was a solid neighbor and decent man. "Tell me what you know," she said.

"This morning's paper. They're rehashing your father's dirty laundry. The second-family story." He glanced away, unable to meet Avery's gaze.

Since that story was old news, Avery just knew there was more. "Gary, please. I'd rather hear it from you than some stranger."

"Come on, hon. Maybe we should go upstairs and let me pull it up on my laptop," Ella said.

"That's a good idea." This from the usually silent Rick.

"No. I'd rather get it over with. What are they saying?"

Gary sighed, obviously resigned. "Stupid, mean things, Avery. Uncalled for and untrue, I'm sure. Things about your father using you to save the daughter he loved more." Gary forced a laugh. "See? Ridiculous."

Not so much, Avery thought. Lights flickered behind her eyes, and she suddenly couldn't breathe well. Anxiety. She drew in deep breaths.

"I mean, anyone who knows you knows how amazing you are. Same with Olivia and your brothers. Of course your father loves you all." He was rambling now.

"Thank you, Gary. We'll read the rest ourselves," Ella said, grabbing Avery's hand and pulling her along.

Avery couldn't believe her father's past was coming back to haunt her again. But it was *her father's* past, she reminded herself. Not anything she'd done. She'd survived the gossip, the talk, the speculation then, and she'd survive it a second time.

They reached the apartment. Rick deposited Ella's suitcase inside and locked the door behind them. "Pack now. I'm getting you ladies out of here," he said.

"No. I want your laptop," she said to Ella.

Rick shot Ella a warning look, but Ella was Avery's best friend. She pulled her computer from her bag. "I think it would be smarter to ignore it."

"And not know what I'm in for the next time a reporter ambushes me? No." Avery settled into a chair in the living room and began tapping on the keys.

She found an article with today's date immediately.

Kingston's Girl Holds On with Iron Grip. She read the headline and winced.

She felt Ella looking over her shoulder. Drawing strength from her friend, Avery read on. After a rehash of Avery's sad past, her father's betrayal of his wife and kids, and the existence of another life and family, the article went on to say that Avery had visited Grey at his Miami concert in the hopes of rekindling their high school romance. Grey had a weak spot for Avery and always had, according to a source who'd asked not to be named.

And because of her past, Avery was too insecure to keep any of the more recent men in her life. They'd managed to get a quote or two from the few guys she'd dated and gently let down. They'd obviously held a grudge or had been paid well, because they claimed she was clingy and needy, all stemming from the daddy issues she had, and they'd been the ones to dump her.

Once she'd gotten her hooks in Grey Kingston, the wealthy, beloved member of Tangled Royal, she held on for all she was worth. She was, in fact, the reason for the breakup of the much-loved band. Again, quoting a source who'd asked not to be named.

"What the ever-loving fuck?" Ella yelled, obviously finishing the offensive article at the same time as Avery.

Avery shook her head, unable to clear the spots that had taken up permanent residence in front of her eyes. Her hands were clammy, her skin damp.

"Avery?"

She heard Ella's voice as if from a distance before she collapsed, everything going dark.

Chapter Twelve

*A*very came to with a cold cloth on her forehead, Ella standing over her with a worried expression on her face.

"I can't believe I passed out."

"Emotional triggers can do that to you," her friend said gently.

"Well, I'm sick and tired of dealing with the emotional fall-out from my past." Avery yanked the cloth off her forehead and struggled to a sitting position.

Ella put a hand on her shoulder. "Stay put until you know you're okay."

Avery brushed at her now-damp hair that stuck to her fore-head. "I feel fine. Can we just forget this ever happened?"

"Umm . . . I don't think so." Ella trailed off and winced. "I called Grey."

"Seriously?"

"I was worried and so was Rick." She glanced over her shoulder at the bodyguard, who stood against the wall, arms folded across his chest. "I didn't want to upset Olivia, her being pregnant, so it was either Grey or one of your brothers. I made a judgment call."

Avery nodded. "I'm not upset with you. I'm angry with myself. I hate that I still let him get to me," she said of her father.

"I have to ask you something." Ella scooted closer on the couch and leaned in so they could speak quietly. "Have you ever had it out with him? Told him how you feel about what he did, how his actions affected your life?"

Avery shook her head. "My mom was my rock, and she made sure I got help. And he wasn't around much, especially right after . . . By the time he tried reaching out to us again, I'd built up all these walls so I couldn't be hurt again."

Ella wrinkled her nose in confusion. "Then why do you go to his birthday party every year?"

Avery sighed. Her father held a yearly birthday bash at The Meridian Hotel, a formal affair for family, friends, and business associates. Avery and her immediate siblings always felt the event was more to show the outside world that things in the Dare family were *fine*, when in reality, all of Avery's full brothers and her sister, Olivia, had their issues with Robert Dare.

"I know it's hard to understand, but I just never wanted Sienna or the others to feel bad for something they'd had no control over." Even if she and Olivia had to twist their brothers' arms, they all made an appearance, usually to support each other.

"I always said you're too good a person," Ella said. "And in this case, I think you need to get those damaging emotions off your chest before you lose the things most precious to you."

Avery's cell rang. Noticing her bag on the table, she pulled out her phone and glanced at the incoming number. "Speak of the devil." She wondered why he'd be calling now. "Might as well get it over with."

She accepted the call. "Hello?"

"Avery, it's your father."

She didn't mention that she'd already figured that out. "Hi, Dad."

"Where are you?" he asked, sounding extremely stressed and unhappy.

"I'm home in my apartment, why?"

"Because we need to talk. I'll be there in about twenty minutes."

"About what?" she asked, but he'd already hung up. She met Ella's concerned gaze. "Guess he's coming to talk."

"Could this day get any weirder?"

Avery shivered, still cold from passing out and uneasy after speaking to her father. Ella rose and grabbed an afghan from the chair across from the sofa and wrapped it around Avery's shoulders.

"Thank you." She snuggled into the warm blanket and scrolled through her phone. "Wow."

"What's up?" Ella asked.

"That wasn't the first time my father called this morning," Avery said, glancing at three missed calls and one voice message with his name on it.

She tapped on the voice mail and played his message out loud.

"Avery, this is your father."

"No shit," Ella muttered, and Avery couldn't help but grin.

Her father continued. "I don't appreciate the fact that your new relationship is dragging up my ancient history, and you need to make this go away. Call me immediately."

"Is he kidding?" Ella asked in disbelief just as a knock sounded at the door and Rick let Grey inside. As Grey entered, Rick turned to her. "I'll be right outside if you need me."

"Thank you."

"And I'll be in my room so you two can talk. But same thing. Yell if you need me," Ella said. "Especially when you-know-who gets here."

Ella and Rick both left them alone.

Grey, looking edible in a pair of jeans and a faded Tangled Royal concert T-shirt, slid onto the couch beside her.

"Are you okay, sugar?" He skimmed his knuckles down her cheek, his green eyes boring into hers.

She didn't realize how much she'd been holding inside her until she heard the concerned tone in his voice, and she broke down. Tears came, unbidden and unwanted, but she couldn't make them stop.

"I'm just so tired of . . . this." She gestured to herself. "I want to be stronger than this. I am stronger than this."

"Crying doesn't make you weak. Your actions are what define you, and you're doing pretty damn good if you ask me."

No, Avery thought. She wasn't. But she would be. "My father called. He's coming to talk. Apparently he's upset that my personal life is bringing up his past indiscretions. Can you imagine that?"

Grey blew out a deep breath, managing to hang onto control by a thread despite the blood pumping hard through his veins. First she was put through the wringer by the press because of him, and now her father was blaming her for it?

"No. And I'll make damn sure he knows if he wants to get to you, he needs to go through me."

She reached out and touched his arm. "It's time I handled my father." Because she believed Ella had had a point earlier. "He needs to know how much damage he's done to me and my life."

Grey didn't like letting her deal with her angry parent, but he respected her need to do it. "I'll be by your side," he said. "That's nonnegotiable."

A smile lifted her lips, and some color finally returned to her face. "Deal."

When he'd walked in, she'd been so pale it'd frightened him. And considering he'd driven here in a panic, ignoring the speed limit to get to her, that was saying something.

"If I were a better man, I'd let you go. I'd settle in LA and make sure that the press and the paparazzi never had a reason to come near you again," he said, the words taking him by surprise.

She narrowed her gaze. "Don't you dare make those kinds of decisions for me."

He appreciated her guts even as guilt swamped him. He'd never wanted the uglier side of his life to touch hers. But he wasn't leaving her.

"Don't worry. I'm not that better man," he said wryly. "I came home and made my play. What kind of fool would I be to walk away from you now?" He chuckled but sobered quickly. "But you're the one suffering from being with me."

"You're wrong, Grey." She grasped his hand tightly and opened her mouth to continue when the doorbell rang. "We're going to have to pick this up later, okay?"

"I'm not going anywhere," he promised her. If she couldn't handle the shit that came with Grey Kingston, she was going to have to be the one to walk away.

The *thought* made his stomach cramp and his heart feel empty, but he refused to dwell on the negative. From everything she'd said and done so far, Avery was willing to step up and fight for them.

Starting with her father.

Avery braced herself as she let her father inside her apartment. She wanted to have a calm, rational, thoughtful conversation with her parent. One that let her explain the things she kept inside and maybe helped forge a new understanding.

"What's with the bodyguard?" he asked, and that one question destroyed any chance for Avery to remain calm, rational, or thoughtful.

Avery blew out a long breath. "Really, Dad? You have eight children, and none of them told you what's going on in my life? Or is it that you only pay attention when something impacts you? Or one of Savannah's kids?" she asked, that last part shocking even Avery.

Robert blinked, obviously startled. "Now, Avery—"

Suddenly, she felt Grey's hand on her shoulder, his strong presence telling her he had her back. A massive lump the size of a boulder formed in her throat, and tears threatened once more. She'd had her mom and her siblings, but until now, this very moment, she'd always felt *alone.*

"Dad, this is Grey Kingston." Avery didn't know if her father remembered her high school boyfriend, and she didn't care.

"I recognize you. And I wish I could say it's a pleasure, but your antics are having a negative impact on my family and my business, young man."

Grey's fingers tightened around her shoulder. "I promised Avery I'd let her deal with you, sir, but make no mistake, if you insult her or hurt her in any way, that promise will mean nothing. So I suggest you tread lightly."

Avery swallowed hard, her heart bursting with emotion and love for this man. She needed him in her life, appreciated how he was inspiring her to fight for herself and, as a result, for them.

"Avery, we need to talk alone."

She shook her head. "No. Grey stays. Say whatever it is you came to say." Then she had words of her own for her father.

"Fine. I want to know what you plan to do about the fact that my old dirty laundry is being dredged up again thanks to your relationship with this man."

She stared at her father and felt very little emotional pull toward him. There were good memories, some holidays, maybe a time or two together as a happy family, until things had fallen apart. But not many, because whenever any of them had needed him, be it for a school event, award, or an illness, he was always working. Or so he'd told them. They'd realized later that working had been a euphemism for being with his other family.

"Avery, I asked you what you plan to do to fix things," he said, his exasperation with her clear.

"Nothing," she told him.

"Excuse me?"

"I don't plan to do a thing. Would you like to know why?" She went on before he could answer. "Because you never gave a damn when your choices impacted me or the rest of the family. One day you came home and blew Mom's world apart. You told her you had another woman you loved and three other kids, and as if that weren't enough, you needed us to be tested for bone marrow to save Sienna's life. And what did Mom do? She agreed!"

Her voice rose and Avery didn't care. She just needed to be heard. Her thoughts and feelings needed to get out of her head and maybe get into his.

"Did you even read what that article said today?" she asked. "Do you care that the whole world now thinks that you used me to save the daughter you loved *more*?"

"Avery," Robert said, his face pale, his voice shaking.

He tried to touch her, and she stepped back into the hard wall of Grey's chest. She trembled inside and out and was grateful for his silent support.

She swallowed hard. "You didn't pick up the phone when a stalker came to my door, you don't care that I'm spearheading this prom for kids with cancer. You aren't proud of me, only of Sienna. And you only think about how these news articles show you in a bad light."

He blinked, his shock genuine as he processed her words. He was that egotistical.

But Avery wasn't finished. "How can you be so surprised? Your actions sucked. Your choices sucked. And after the truth came out, you didn't do anything to make it better for *us*. Your first family." She was shaking now, and Grey wrapped his arms around her, keeping her secure. Safe. "Do you realize you never thanked me for what I did for Sienna? And I don't care. I don't need or want your thanks. But back then, I needed and wanted *you*."

"I was so wrapped up in Sienna's illness, in her having cancer, I didn't think—"

"That's the problem," she said, her voice breaking. "You don't think. You have no idea how that time period impacted me. My life." She drew a deep breath. "My *sanity*."

Before Robert could react, Grey eased her into his side and faced her father. "I think that's enough. Avery's had a rough day, and I'm calling a stop to this."

"He's right," Avery said. "If you want to talk, call me, and maybe we can get together when this mess has died down and I'm calmer." Not that she was holding her breath.

Ian had told her that their father had apologized to him once and encouraged him not to make the kind of mistakes he had in life. But clearly Robert hadn't learned from his own past.

"I love you and your brothers and sister. I didn't know," he said again.

Avery shook her head. "That's just it. You didn't know. But you also never bothered to ask or find out." Avery dropped into the nearest chair as Grey let her father out, feeling lighter for finally having expressed her feelings to the one man who'd set the bar for all the pain and agony in her life.

Grey returned to her and knelt by her feet. "Sugar, you have no idea how proud I am."

"Thanks. I'm feeling . . . pretty good myself." Her adrenaline was riding high now, and she wanted to take advantage.

She grasped Grey's hand. "I have an idea, and it's going to sound crazy. But I have the press's ear now, right?"

He met her gaze warily. "Right . . . ?"

The idea had come to her as she'd been yelling at her father about the event and her role in it. "I want to use that attention to raise money for the cancer center at the hospital. I don't care if they think I'm using you or keeping you with me because I'm so needy I can't be alone. We know the truth, right?"

A beat of silence lay heavily between them before Grey asked, "What is the truth?" He sounded uncertain, and her heart twisted for all the pain she'd inadvertently caused him while trying to protect herself.

He'd stepped up from the beginning, while she'd been hesitant and unsure. She'd never expressed her feelings, not even after he had.

She met his gaze and held on, looking into his eyes. "I love you, Grey Kingston. I always have. And if I've handled everything thrown at me in the last few weeks, I think the future can only get easier."

If eyes could truly lighten in color, his did. A slow, easy smile spread over his handsome face, and as she put her heart completely into his hands, she saw he would take the very best care of it. And her.

"I love you too, Very." He kissed her nose and the side of her lips before devouring her mouth and lingering long enough for her to drown in his taste and scent.

He broke the kiss, his hands cupped around her cheeks. "I loved you when we were eighteen, but when I met you again, I fell even harder. You understand me, and you make me want to be a better man. Less selfish, less concerned about the outside world, and more focused on you. And family. The things that matter, that I lost sight of for too long."

She grasped his hands. "You've done the same for me. You made me want to push past the fears that bound me for my entire life. I faced my father for the first time, and I feel . . . free." She wasn't stupid. She didn't think that just because she'd expressed her feelings to her father her anxiety was gone for good. But she did believe she was more equipped to handle it now. And most importantly, she wasn't running. "I'm here for the long haul. Whatever that may be."

Before he could answer, Ella called out, "Is the ogre gone?" Her laughter broke the intensity of the moment.

"Later," Grey whispered, his gaze holding onto hers. "We'll define that long haul later."

Her heart skipped a beat, and she nodded, finally ready for whatever life had to offer.

Grey didn't trust silence. Especially when that silence came from Simon Colson. Over the next few weeks, things fell into place neatly. Almost too neatly, and Grey was nervous.

First Dawn Mills replied to his message and, through her representative, issued a statement along with pages from her deceased husband's diary. All confirmed that Grey Kingston had done more than cowrite the album with Alden Mills.

While her husband had been extremely ill, Grey had done most of the work on their collaboration, including writing the lyrics. Simon didn't have another salvo, and he'd stopped messing with Grey's life.

Whoever had defaced Avery's apartment door hadn't resurfaced. Ella moved back into their apartment, but Avery remained with Grey. Tyler demanded a bodyguard remain with each woman, and Grey insisted on covering costs. He didn't trust Simon's silence any more than he believed the stalker was a one-time thing.

But life went on, and Alden's words from the grave turned Grey into even more of an icon than he had already been. Offers for collaboration and requests for him to write lyrics were piling up, so he had finally given in and hired a new agent to help him sort through things.

Every day, he expected Avery to freak out and think he'd find a reason to leave town, but she was steady. As a rock. True to her word, the day after the confrontation with her father, she'd asked Grey to contact a reporter he trusted to put the correct spin on a story. And together, they'd sat down for an interview.

She'd held his hand and told how her experience as a bone marrow donor as a young girl had led her to volunteer her time with the patients at the hospital today. She elaborated on the prom and explained how she'd like to do various events for the kids throughout the year, but the hospital lacked funds. And when Avery Dare, with Grey Kingston by her side, asked for money for the kids, contributions poured in.

The largest donor to the now-named Dare Fund for Kids was Robert Dare. His financial contribution was substantial . . . and promised yearly. And though Avery and her father's relationship was by no means solid, the man was making an effort, and Avery was trying to meet him halfway.

As for Avery, between filming her upcoming videos, some of which she decided to do outdoors, and working on the prom, she had little time for worry. She did, however, make plenty of time for Grey. And he couldn't deny that things between them had never been better. Which was why he'd planned his surprise as tonight's main event.

The rest of his life hinged on this evening. And Grey Kingston, who performed in front of hundreds of thousands and was never nervous, had a raging case of stage fright.

Avery spent the entire afternoon setting up at the hospital, and she couldn't wait to see the end result tonight. The normally staid, often sad hospital floor and its doctors, nurses, patients, and volunteers were buzzing with contagious excitement. Thanks to pressure from the kids, Avery and Ella agreed to dress up in gowns too. Avery left the kids with the makeup artists and hairstylists so she could go home and change.

She stood in Grey's bedroom and straightened his bow tie, resisting the urge to undress him, button by button. The desire to pull this handsome man onto the bed and have her wicked way with him was strong, but they couldn't miss the whole evening. One last tug on his tie and she finished and stepped away, heading into the bathroom to fix her makeup and put on her dress.

The door was open, so she talked to Grey as she touched up her mascara. "I'm so happy you invited your parents tonight. And they're not just attending, they're working."

"They can't wait," he said.

She had planned to stay late and clean up, but to her surprise, Grey had arranged for his parents to come help with the setup, serving, and cleanup at the end. He tried to play down the significance, but Avery knew better.

"It's a big deal, you asking them to help with the serving and cleaning. To know you are proud of them for who they are. Your mom cried," Avery said, remembering the phone call from Susie.

Grey strode into the bathroom just as Avery had undressed. She stood in her barely there bra and panties, a formal white Grecian style dress hanging behind her.

"Something I can do for you?" she asked, sounding cheeky. And happy.

Because she was. Happier than she'd ever been. Yes, the photographers who had found out where she and Grey were and snapped pictures still sometimes freaked her out. But she was learning to ignore what the papers, online and print, and blogs had to say. She'd canceled her "Tangled Royal" and "Grey Kingston" Google Alerts so she wouldn't see things that weren't true and would only upset her. Her anxiety wasn't miraculously gone, nor had she thought it would be.

Again, she was dealing. She'd made an appointment to discuss her medications, and she still hoped she could cut down one day soon. And if dealing with her father occasionally made her crazy, the money he'd donated to her cause was more than worth it. As was putting a childhood's worth of pain behind her.

"Grey?" she asked, meeting his heated gaze in the mirror as he stood behind her. "Do you want something?"

"For you to grab the counter, bend over, and let me have my way with you." He cocked an eyebrow and practically devoured her with his gaze.

She bent over as directed and wiggled her ass his way before straightening. "Sorry, but we have to get going. Can you hand me my dress?" she asked, doing her best to sound unaffected.

But the truth was, she wished they did have time, because now she was wet, and her desire to feel him hot and thick inside her had been growing since seeing him looking all devastating in his tux.

He let out a low growl. "You will pay for that little tease later."

"Promise?" She leaned over and kissed his cheek, inhaling the smell of his aftershave—and him.

Before she could dance out of the way, he grasped her waist and pulled her to him, her nearly naked body brushing against his formally clad one. The thick fabric did nothing to hide his massive erection, and it was an erotic feeling, being undressed and desired while he was fully clothed.

His fingers trailed up from her waist until his thumbs brushed the underside of her breasts.

She trembled and felt her nipples pucker into hard and needy points. That white dress was going to give people one hell of a show unless she got herself under control.

Without warning, he slid his hands back to her waist.

She moaned her complaint and he grinned. "I need you focused and that wasn't helping," he said.

"What is it?" she asked.

He tipped her head back and looked into her eyes. "Before things get crazy tonight, I wanted to make sure you knew how proud I am of you. You've come so far in such a short time when it comes to us, and you put together not just a prom for seriously ill children, you formed an entire *fund* for their benefit."

His words and approval warmed her, but she didn't know how to explain the recent changes. "I'd been feeling that growing need to get over the past so I could move forward with you. Then I fainted, and when I came to I was just . . . so tired of being emotionally crippled."

He shook his head. "That is too strong a description. You had every right to be wary of me and my life."

She didn't want to argue. "Fine, but the thing that gave me the final push in the end was that I realized I wanted something so badly I couldn't imagine living without it."

A pleased smile lifted his sexy lips. "What would that be?" he asked in a gruff voice.

That question had an easy answer. "Us," she murmured. "I wanted us."

He kissed her hard, turned her around, and pulled her panties down her legs. It was fast, loving, and oh so necessary. Especially when he came inside her, shouting out not just her name but a gruff *I love you* before collapsing against her.

They made it to the party in the nick of time.

Chapter Thirteen

alfway through the night, Avery counted the event a success. The room was decorated in blue and gold, the colors chosen by the kids in a poll done by the nursing staff during their rounds. The Mylar balloons and streamers, along with matching plates and silverware, tablecloths, cups, and almost everything else had been provided by a local company that Sienna had arm-twisted into a full donation, not just a discounted rate. She was a true Dare when it came to getting what she wanted, Avery thought.

And everything was documented for posterity. Thanks to the interview she'd done to draw attention to her cause, a local photographer had reached out and offered to take pictures of the event and provide copies to the families free of charge.

Music sounded from an iPod speaker system, the songs also chosen by the attendees. Avery made sure to spend time with each of the children, complimenting them on their formal wear, talking to them, and finding out how they were enjoying the night. But by far, her favorite part of the evening was introducing Grey to the kids and watching their eyes open wide with wonder and excitement.

He, like Lola, who had surprised her by arriving along with her promised gifts, spent time with them all. Avery couldn't remember a time when her heart was fuller.

Almost every member of her family had made a brief appearance, offering their love, hugs, and support. Her mother was the first to arrive along with her fiancé, Michael Brooks, and the last to leave. None of her siblings lingered, understanding that the night was about the children. But knowing they cared enough to stop by warmed every part of Avery's heart.

"Avery, a word?"

She turned at the sound of her father's voice, the one family member she hadn't yet seen. "Dad. I—" She stopped herself before saying, *I wondered if you'd show up.* "I'm glad you're here," she said instead.

"I know I haven't been much of a father, and I'm sorry you had to spell it out for me that way. But—"

Avery didn't want anything marring this night, least of all another conversation about something that was in the past. "It's over. I'd like it if we could just move forward from here."

He exhaled sharply and nodded, clearly relieved to have been given a reprieve. "This is fabulous," he said. "You've done a terrific thing for these kids."

He met her gaze, and in his eyes, she saw he meant it.

"Thank you," she murmured.

"Where's your man?" he asked.

Avery looked toward the far side of the room, where she'd seen Grey last, with Lilly, the youngest patient there, who couldn't leave her wheelchair.

"I'm not sure. Why?" she asked, suddenly wary.

Her father shifted from foot to foot. "I thought maybe I could start over. Get to know him."

Avery raised her eyebrows in surprise. "I'd like that."

Before she could say more, a commotion sounded from outside the room, and Avery realized she needed to take care of it before something disrupted the kids' fun.

"I have to go see what's going on." She headed for the exit, her father close behind.

She pushed through the double doors and saw Rick with Ella's bodyguard, Jack Tantor, detaining a redheaded woman.

The two men had been assigned to keep guard outside the main room. Marco, Grey's bodyguard, was posted outside the hospital's front entrance.

As she approached, she realized Grey stood in the circle of men, and she met his horrified gaze.

"He's mine!" the woman shrieked, her red hair a frizzy mess, her breasts practically popping out of her barely there top.

Avery stepped closer, her gaze drawn to faded black writing on the woman's chest. "Is that—Oh my God! Your name is on her breast!" she said to Grey, appalled.

His cheeks flamed a healthy shade of red.

"I told you he's mine. I warned you to break up with him or else!" The redhead dove for Avery.

Avery flinched, but she was safe.

Rick held the woman tight.

"Cops are on their way," Jack said. "Marco will meet them at the door and fill them in."

Avery stared, the woman's words buzzing in her head until suddenly they coalesced and made sense. "You warned me?" she repeated. "You broke into my building? Wrote on my door? Forced me to move out of my home?" Avery asked, her voice rising as she faced the person responsible for the upheaval in her life.

"Grey's mine!" she spat back.

"The hell he is," Avery replied.

"Avery, get inside," Grey ordered, stepping toward her.

"Not happening." She glared at the crazy woman and squared her shoulders. She was finished cowering, fainting, and anything else that involved not coping with her life.

The elevator doors opened, and uniformed officers strode out, handcuffs ready.

Crazy Lady took one look at the cuffs and screamed. "No! I'm not going down for this alone. He promised me Grey would be mine. He said all I had to do was scare the little blonde chick and everything would be fine!" She cried and broke down in sobs and tears.

Grey stepped in front of Avery, but she peeked around him, not wanting to miss a thing.

"*He* who?" Grey yanked the woman's arms away from her now-makeup-stained face. "Who made those promises?" he asked, his voice harsh and biting.

To her surprise, her father stood beside her, pulling her away from the insanity. Protecting her.

"The British guy," the woman wailed.

"Simon Colson?" Grey asked as the cops pushed him aside.

"Yes, that's him. He helped me with the blog comments and told me where she lived." She pointed a shaking hand at Avery. "He promised if I did what he said, Grey would be mine. He bugged your phone, told the press where to find you. And now it's all going to be okay. Tonight is about us, baby," she said to him, clearly delusional.

Simon had merely fed her fantasies for his own purposes, and it made Avery sick to her stomach.

"Can't you see we're meant to be?" She sniffed and pointed to the faded writing on her chest. "Remember that day? You couldn't stop staring! They're yours!"

"Eew," Avery muttered, turning away. She was really ready to get back to the kids and let the cops deal with the crazy.

She turned away, her heart pounding hard in her chest. She had no doubt the woman would be arrested, and with luck, they'd be able to find Simon and take him in as well. More important things were going on behind those doors, Avery thought.

And as she headed back inside to the party, she realized she'd stayed strong. She hadn't come close to fainting. She wasn't threatened by Grey's crazy fan nor did she feel the urge to run away. More progress, she thought. Now if she could just stop thinking about Grey's signature on that woman's boobs, she'd be even better.

After the police hauled Emerald away in handcuffs and promised to pick up Simon for questioning, Grey had every intention of finding Avery. Her expression after listening to Emerald's ranting and, worse, seeing his signature on her chest, stayed with him. Remorse and regret building stronger all the time.

He couldn't change his past, but he'd definitely changed his future, and he needed to make sure Avery still believed that. He couldn't have all they'd built—were still building—wiped away on a night when he'd planned . . .

"Grey?" Lola's voice cut off his thoughts.

"Yeah?"

She walked over to where he stood in the hallway and hooked her arm in his. "You okay?"

"Not really."

"Rick filled me in on what went down. I'm so sorry. If I could get my hands on Simon . . ."

"He's finished in the industry, and I hope they'll find charges that'll keep him tied up for a good long while." But Grey didn't want to think about the man anymore. "Is Rep here?"

Lola nodded. "He went inside. I wanted to talk to you. Are we still a go?"

He patted his tuxedo pants pocket, glanced at Lola, and nodded. "We are." His chances for a yes to the biggest question of his life, however, had just plummeted exponentially. But he still had to try.

Sweat poured off Grey's body, and his heart beat a too-rapid rhythm as Ella whistled and the room of expectant faces peered up at her in curiosity. From where Grey watched from the corner of the room, even Avery's nose wrinkled in confusion. All part of the surprise, he thought, his pulse racing too fast.

"Ladies and gentlemen," Ella said with a grin at the kids, "we have a surprise for you tonight. Two very special people are here to sing for you. Let's give a big round of applause to Lola Corbin and Grey Kingston of the band Tangled Royal!"

Ella clapped, and the crowd burst into applause and happy screams.

Rep, who'd been waiting in the corner, handed Grey his guitar, and for the next half hour, he and Lola performed for the kids. Those who could dance did. Those who couldn't sat and listened or sang along, smiles on their too-pale faces. No performance had ever meant or affected Grey more, because no audience had ever appreciated the moment quite as much. Because they knew, as most didn't, that time wasn't promised, and enjoying life when they could truly mattered.

When he and Lola had planned this, it'd felt small and inconsequential. There was so little he could do to add to what Avery had accomplished tonight, but giving sick kids a great memory to keep with them and share with their friends allowed him to play a small part. Now he understood the reasons she volunteered and what she got out of the time she spent here. He wanted to continue to do his small part to make kids like these smile.

He and Lola wrapped their miniset, and he ran a hand through his damp hair. The high that always came with performing still pulsed through his veins, only tonight, there was so much more emotion attached to it. Avery had always been in his vision and thoughts during the performance. His beautiful angel, looking fucking perfect and representing everything he wanted, wrapped in a white gown and warm smile. But while he had no doubt she'd loved his contribution, whether she still loved him enough to stay with him remained to be seen. He'd marred her perfect charitable event with his fame. The same fame she had run from before.

He drew a breath for courage and looked her way. She stood beside a young, pale girl in a wheelchair, an IV attached to her arm. Her focus was on the child, who couldn't dance, participate, or do more than sit and take things in, and as Grey looked at them, he lost his heart to her all over again.

His mouth dry, he walked over and knelt down so he was at Lilly's eye level. "How are you, gorgeous? Having fun?" he asked the ten-year-old he'd met earlier.

Her wig had tilted a little on her head, but she nodded, her eyes bright. Behind her, her parents held hands, smiling down at their daughter.

Grey cleared his throat, unable to speak just yet.

The girl looked up at him. "You were really awesome," she told him in an embarrassed whisper.

He ducked his head. "Thanks. That's because I had someone special in the audience watching me." He winked at the girl, and she grinned.

"This was the best night," she told him.

"I think so too. I hope it's going to get even better. Is it okay if I steal Avery here for a minute? I need to ask her something very important."

Lilly nodded. "I promised my parents they could take me back to my room so I could rest. Thank you for the best night," she said again.

"Anytime," he told her. Heart in his throat, Grey rose to his feet and met Avery's gaze.

Her luminous violet eyes were filled with moisture. He wasn't sure if she was happy, sad, or a combination of both.

"Come with me?" He extended his hand, knowing his entire future hinged on her answer.

He grasped her hand, relieved when she didn't pull away, and led her to a quiet corner of the room. He'd planned a big spectacle, but Emerald's appearance had killed that idea. And he hadn't had time to corner her before his performance.

He held both her hands in his and met her gaze. Words normally came easy, but his brain felt scattered and his heart fragile. Only this woman could do this to him, Grey thought.

He met her gaze and forged ahead. "I'm so damned sorry the craziness in my life has to touch you at all, but especially tonight." He shook his head and groaned.

Her lips lifted a little. "I think we already established the crazy comes with your rock star status," she said, her words not giving him a lick of insight into her feelings. "You signed her boobs?" she asked him.

He winced. Of all the questions or comments he thought she'd have about tonight, that hadn't been it. Hell, he'd been trying to put those kinds of things out of his mind for years.

"I'm not proud of it, but it came with the territory. Avery—"

"Do you realize how long it's been since she showered if she still had your name on her chest?" she asked, her voice rising.

Once again, his mind hadn't gone there either, and he cringed. "I'd rather not think about it," he muttered.

"Me neither. I could have lived the rest of my life without knowing or seeing that." She wrinkled her nose in adorable disgust.

"Avery," he tried again. "I could live the rest of my life without all of it. I just can't live it without you."

He revealed his heart and finally captured her full attention, her eyes huge on his.

"Oh, Grey."

He grasped her hands tighter. She was his lifeline, and he wasn't letting go. "I couldn't stand it if you walked away from me now, after we've gone through so much and come out the other side."

Before she could reply, he slid his hand into his pocket and pulled out the ring he'd bought way before he'd ever had a realistic chance with her but long after he'd gotten to know her.

"I realize I left you once, but I promise never again. And I know I'm not a bargain, and I bring with me more hassle than you need or want in your life, but I love you. I want to take care of you, to have fun with you, and to be by your side for the rest of my life."

She blinked back what he prayed were happy tears.

He held out the ring and went on, putting it all on the line. Because that's what he'd done when he'd left her behind years ago, seeking that shot at fame and fortune in LA. He'd been lucky once, and he prayed the stars aligned for him again.

"The box wouldn't fit in my pocket." He held the delicate ring between his thumb and forefinger. "It's a mix of traditional and modern . . . it's Tiffany," he said, letting out a nervous laugh. "And it's you."

Avery stared at the gorgeous engagement ring, looking so delicate in Grey's big tanned hands. He was right; the halo style, cushion cut encircled by double rows of bead-set diamonds, with a diamond band was the perfect mix of traditional and modern. And it *was* perfect for her.

"So? Will you marry me, sugar?"

Her legs began to shake, and somehow she managed to nod and not pass out, this time for the very best reasons. "Yes, yes, I'll marry you."

"Thank fuck," he muttered and slid the ring onto her finger.

Laughing, she flung her arms around his neck and breathed in everything that was Grey. With a happy groan, he raised her into his arms and hugged her tight.

"No more signing boobs," she whispered in his ear.

"Not even yours?" he asked.

A sudden swell of applause cut off any snappy retort she might have had, and she realized they had an audience. A very young, very excited audience who'd just witnessed their rock star idol proposing.

She shook her head at him and laughed. "You're a dirty thinker, Grey Kingston. And I love you."

"Love you more," he said right back, and in front of their young crowd, he bent her backward and kissed her for all she was worth.

The Dare to Love Series continues
with Dare to Take, Book #6

Dare to Love Series

Turn the page to start reading the *Dare to Take* excerpt!

Chapter One

The sun shone overhead, the temperature neared ninety, and the humidity was hair-curlingly high on the Caribbean island of St. Lucia, making it hard to believe a hurricane was coming soon. Ella Shaw glanced up at the blue sky, knowing it wouldn't remain pristine for long.

The calm before the storm.

She pulled her hair into a high ponytail and headed out of her hotel, determined to hit the local gift shop she'd caught sight of on her way to the photo shoot yesterday. She'd seen long, draping, blue-beaded necklaces from the storefront window, but she hadn't had time to stop. Her boss was a stickler for getting the right shot in the exact light, and they'd worked well past dark. By the time they'd wrapped for the day, the store had been closed.

As an assistant for Angie Crighton, a fashion designer based in Miami, Ella was responsible for the little details involved in a photo shoot. And though Angie, the photographer, and models had left the island this morning, Ella had stayed to make sure the shooting site was clean, the hotel pleased enough to allow them back another time. And if she were honest with herself, she liked the downtime after the craziness of a photo shoot, the rushing around of the crew, and the bossiness of some of the models and, of course, of Angie herself.

Ella appreciated the fact that she had time to souvenir shop for her best friend, Avery Dare. How ironic was it that the two girls from very different worlds had met at all? But they had. And it was Avery who'd introduced Ella to the finer things in life, leading her to seek out a job with an haute-couture designer. Whereas Avery came from a wealthy family, Ella had been raised firmly middle class, but the two girls had bonded instantly. They'd even shared an apartment until recently, when her best friend had moved in with her rock star fiancé, Grey Kingston.

Yep, two different worlds, even now, Ella thought wryly. But their friendship was solid. Which reminded her, she needed to let Avery know she might not make it back to the States tomorrow as planned.

When Ella had heard about the storm changing course, she'd tried to book an earlier flight out without success. She shivered at the possibility of being stranded here alone during a hurricane and knew Avery would like the news even less. Her best friend suffered from severe anxiety, and Ella didn't like to make her worry.

She'd just buy Avery an extra gift to make up for it, she thought, walking into the shop. She immediately headed to the turquoise-blue beads she'd seen through the window. The shopkeeper claimed they were Larimar beads. Even if they were fake, the beads, popular in the Caribbean, were said to have healing powers. Ella purchased two dozen, a mix of bracelets and necklaces, so she could share with the children at the cancer treatment center where she and Avery volunteered.

Avery had been nine and Ella ten years old when they'd met at a Miami hospital, both donating bone marrow, both there at the behest of a parent. Neither of them really understanding what was happening. All Ella had known was that she was doing a favor for her father, helping the stepmother Ella didn't like all that much to begin with. Even at a young age, Ella had been a good judge of character, a better one than her father, obviously, because shortly after Janice had gotten well, she'd left Ella's dad. And both her father and Ella's life had gone downhill from there. Ella shook off the thoughts of her past before she could go deeper and darker, and focused on the pretty jewelry.

She spent some time choosing a thick turquoise bracelet for Avery and a similar one for herself before paying for everything and waiting for the shopkeeper to wrap things up.

Bag in hand, she started back to the hotel, cutting through side streets and looking into the windows of the stores, soaking up the culture along the cobblestone streets before heading back to Miami tomorrow. At least, she still hoped she'd be home. Knowing she couldn't change the outcome, she pushed her worrisome thoughts aside. She'd deal with the situation as it came.

Sweat dampened her neck from the humidity of the island, and she contemplated taking a cab back to the hotel. She reached into her straw bag and pulled out her cell phone to make the call, when, without warning, she felt a hard jerk on her purse.

"What the—?" She spun around, but whoever wanted her purse was quicker.

She barely caught a glimpse of a tall guy with dark hair as he yanked harder, nearly pulling her shoulder out of its socket before slamming her against the nearby building with his other hand.

Her head hit the concrete wall, and spots immediately appeared behind her eyes from the impact. As she struggled not to pass out, the man grabbed her purse, along with her cell phone that had fallen to the ground.

She opened her mouth to scream, but nothing came out. Her legs collapsed beneath her, and she fell to the ground, her head smacking the sidewalk before everything went black.

Tyler Dare had a full day planned, a packed schedule of appointments with existing and potential clients of Double

Down Security, the firm he now co-owned with his brother Scott. Serena Gibson, his close friend and personal assistant, had strict orders not to let anyone interrupt him this morning so he could pull together his notes for each meeting.

He picked up the threat assessment sheet for his first client, a diplomat who needed protection for his family, and had begun to scan the findings when he heard raised voices.

"I'm sorry, Avery, but he said no interruptions," Serena insisted.

"That's okay, I'm sure he'll see me." His sister's voice carried through the closed office door.

"Avery, he said not to let anyone inside." Serena's voice rose, but he knew the soft-spoken woman was no match for a determined Dare female.

Sure enough, his door swung open, and Avery barreled inside, Serena a step behind her. "Sorry, Tyler."

He waved her worry away. "It's fine."

"Thank you, Serena," Avery said in a sweet voice. "I'll buy you coffee one day soon."

"Make it a martini and you're on," Serena muttered, heading back to her desk.

Tyler knew the other woman meant it. She was a single mom, raising her young daughter alone after her husband had . . . died. Tyler pushed thoughts of Jack Gibson to the far recesses of his mind. Going there meant reliving way too much pain. Pain he'd left behind him when he'd departed from the army.

Instead, he turned to his sister, and with a groan, he rose to his feet. "Couldn't you have called first? I'm swamped today. And what if I was in a meeting?"

Avery rolled her eyes . . . and why not? When she wanted to get her way, she did. She and Olivia, their sister, were typical Dares, stubborn and headstrong, just like him.

She strode over and placed both hands on his face, meeting his gaze. "Family comes first, isn't that what you always told me?"

A distinct edgy tingle raced up his spine. Quoting his words back at him meant she wanted something.

But she had a point. Ever since their father had announced he had another family, moved out, and divorced their mother, his oldest brother, Ian, along with Tyler and Scott, had circled around their sisters and mother. Nothing was more important than family. Even if Tyler still felt like he'd been a coconspirator in betraying them all, having walked in on his father and his mistress when he'd visited his dad at work a year before everyone's life had imploded.

His father had guilted him into keeping his secret. "You don't want to be responsible for your mother's pain, son. Be a man. Keep my secret."

As an adult, Tyler understood Robert Dare was responsible for everyone's pain. But as a kid, all he'd wanted to do was protect the mother he adored . . . and be a man, as his father had said.

All conflicting, fucked-up feelings for a kid to handle. So he hadn't handled it at all. He'd kept the old man's secrets, never admitting the truth, not even to Ian or Scott, and in doing so, he lived with the knowledge that, had he spoken up, he could have spared his mother the humiliation of how she'd found out. When his father had approached her with the painful demand that all her children be tested as bone marrow donors for one of his other kids. Because when things got emotionally difficult, Tyler ran. And that hadn't been the only time.

"Tyler, are you okay?" Avery asked, placing a hand on his arm.

"Fine." He shook off the past. "What's up?" he asked, focusing completely on what his sister wanted.

"It's about Ella."

His dick immediately perked up at the name. "Ella."

Avery narrowed those violet eyes in confusion. "Yes, Ella."

"Ella," he repeated, his brain flickering with images he'd long sought to expunge from memory. A lithe body with pert breasts, warm, silken skin covering his own.

"You know, Ella Shaw," his sister said, breaking into his memories. "My best friend."

And the woman whose virginity he'd taken when she was eighteen.

Yes, Tyler knew exactly who Ella was. It was just that every time he saw her face or heard her name, his brain short-circuited and a mixture of self-loathing and guilt threatened to crush him, followed immediately by a shock of arousal he had no right to feel.

"What's wrong with her?" Tyler asked, already turning his attention back to the day ahead, potential clients he wanted to acquire, new security systems he thought existing clients should agree to upgrade to.

Whatever issues Ella had, Tyler felt certain she didn't need him to handle them. Avery was overreacting. She had to be.

He made it a distinct point to keep as far from Ella Shaw as possible. It was better for both of them to pretend that night had never happened, and by silent, mutual agreement, they'd managed to keep that mistake from Avery.

Avery slammed her hands on his desk, bringing his focus back to the situation at hand. "Ella was mugged in the Caribbean. She's in the hospital with a concussion, her passport is gone, along with everything in her purse, and a hurricane is headed straight for St. Lucia."

Shit, shit, shit. "Is she okay?" he asked, more concerned than he wanted to admit.

"I don't know. She sounded groggy. The nurse wouldn't let her stay on the phone, but Ty, she can't leave the island without proper documents, and all her identification is gone. She can't get to the American Embassy since they won't release her from the hospital for another twenty-four hours because she's alone. And when she is released, the hurricane will have hit and—" Avery didn't get another word out because she started to hyperventilate.

Tyler recognized the signs. She'd been suffering from panic attacks since she was a kid, and though they were mostly under control now, truly stressful situations caused an attack.

"Come on. Sit." He wrapped an arm around her shoulders and led her to a chair, easing her down. "Do you have your Xanax?" She nodded and, though still breathing fast, began to look through her purse.

"Serena, I need a glass of water, quick!" Tyler called out to his secretary.

She rushed in a few seconds later, a cup of water in hand.

"Thanks," he said.

Avery took the pill and began to do breathing exercises.

"Can I get you anything else?" Serena asked.

He shook his head, his focus on Avery. "We're good for now."

Serena quickly stepped out, shutting the door behind her.

"Okay, look," Tyler said, kneeling by his sister's side. "You're going to write down where she is, and I'll contact the embassy. I'll do what I can to get her out."

"You have to go yourself. Please. I need to know Ella is okay and with someone I trust after all she's been through." She grasped his hand and squeezed tight. "Ian will let you take his jet. Private is the only way she can fly out without a passport anyway."

She gazed up at him with the same big eyes he'd been a sucker for when she was a kid. Except this time she had no idea what she was asking of him, as the past came flooding back.

He'd come home on leave from the army just in time for Christmas. As usual, Ella had been visiting for the holiday. And holy shit, she was hot. Her body had filled out, with sexy tits and sweet curvy hips; she'd knocked him on his ass. For the first time, he'd seen her as a beautiful woman and not his little sister's best friend, and he'd had to remind himself many times over the course of the night she was off-limits.

Except nobody had given Ella the memo.

In hindsight, he should have seen she'd had a crush on him for years, but she'd just been the kid he looked out for, the little girl he'd met when she was donating bone marrow to her stepmom. He'd always felt protective of her, mostly because she was such a little thing for so long.

Once he'd enlisted, his trips home were sporadic, and he hadn't seen Ella in years. Not until that night.

"Tell me you're on fucking birth control," Tyler had said to a very naked, beautiful, and obviously vulnerable Ella. But he'd been too angry with himself and, at the time, with her, to see it.

She'd managed a nod, her brown hair hanging over her bare shoulder, her hazel eyes a damp mossy-green. "I am."

Relief had flooded him. She might have crawled into his bed uninvited, but he'd known damn well what he was doing when he'd thrust inside her. She'd been so damned tight, and when he'd hit that obvious barrier, he'd realized immediately . . . but it was too late. His control had snapped, and he'd taken her hard and fast, nothing like what her first time should have been like—and would have, if he'd been sober. If he'd known she was a virgin. But if he hadn't been drunk, she wouldn't have made it into his bed in the first place.

"It's okay." She'd reached out and touched his bare chest, the sweet gesture a brand on his skin, and his body had woken up again, hardening for her. Which had only served to piss him off more.

"No, it isn't okay. It was a big fucking mistake. A mess, and you better believe it won't be happening again."

Tears had filled her eyes as she'd gathered her clothes, pulled her long shirt on, and had run, slamming his bedroom door behind her.

"Fuck." He'd fallen back against the pillows, so furious at himself he couldn't think straight.

Traveling to the Caribbean to rescue Ella would bring them alone together for the first time since he'd looked her in the eye and spoken with all the finesse of a drunk twenty-three-year-old.

He'd been an ass. Worse, he hadn't stuck around the next day to apologize. He'd kissed his mother good-bye and lied, saying he'd been called back to base, all to avoid facing Ella. And in the years since, he hadn't manned up any better. He ran a hand through his hair, now longer than regulation length. If any man had treated his sisters the way he'd treated Ella, Tyler would have had their balls.

"Ty? You'll go get her, right? What if it's worse than a concussion and they misdiagnosed her? She needs someone there before the storm hits."

He groaned, already having come to the same conclusion. "Yeah. She does." He grabbed a pen and paper from his desk and handed it to Avery. "Write down everything you know about where she's staying and what hospital she's in. I'll call Ian and have him get in touch with his pilot."

"Umm, plane's fueled and ready," she said, a flush staining her cheeks.

Tyler shook his head. "That sure of me, hmm?"

"You're a good guy, Tyler. Plus you're the best at what you do. If anyone can handle things for Ella, I know you can."

Oh man. Talk about more guilt. If Avery knew about his past with her best friend, she wouldn't be sending him down to take care of her. But he couldn't worry about what Avery would or wouldn't think. He had to make sure Ella was okay, and to do that, he needed to check the weather forecasts and hope like hell he could get onto the small island before the storm.

The flight had been bumpy, and by the time Tyler landed, the wind was whipping through the trees. His goal was to get Ella settled safely into the hotel before the hurricane hit. He arrived at the hospital to find pure chaos. Unlike an American-run place, with generators and general preparedness, the staff was more concerned with getting themselves home than with the welfare of their patients.

He stopped a few people before someone, finally, directed him to the American woman down the hall. Considering she'd been mugged, the fact that they didn't ask him for ID or worry that maybe he was out to hurt her concerned him. It made him all the more determined to get her out of there as soon as possible.

During the trip down, he hadn't stopped to ask himself why he was doing this. He'd said no to his sister before. Not often, but he managed when he wanted to. So why put himself in the position of rescuing a woman he had such a messy history with? One who surely wouldn't be happy to see him, and whom he'd have no choice but to apologize to?

And there he had his answer. He'd let her down, and she wasn't the first person in his life he'd disappointed when they needed him, and he was trying to make amends and correct his past mistakes.

Tyler, like all of his siblings, had idolized their father, Robert Dare. After his other life and family had come to light, he'd shattered each child in different ways.

Ian had stepped up and taken over as man of the house. Sure, Tyler and Scott had helped look after their sisters, but it was Ian who'd held them together. And by taking care of the family, Ian had made sure Scott could be a cop and Tyler could do what he wanted with his life.

And what had Tyler done? Instead of facing the anger he felt at his father, Tyler had run away, joining the army, telling himself it was a big FU to his dad. In reality, it was a cowardly act of betrayal to his family. And when he'd come home on leave and treated Ella so badly, had he faced her the next day? No, he thought, combing a hand through his hair. He'd run again.

He wasn't ready to delve back into how he'd learned these lessons courtesy of Jack Gibson, who'd bailed on his family, on life, in the worst possible way. Tyler visited that in his nightmares often enough. But learn them he had. And if Ella's mugging and the damned hurricane gave him the chance to make things right, he would. He owed her a lot more than an apology.

For the last nine years, he hadn't been able to get the night with Ella or the morning after out of his head. Now was his chance to make it up to her and get rid of some of the guilt he'd been carrying around for being a dick.

For calling her a mistake.

For a lot of things.

He walked down the hall and stopped outside the room he'd been directed to. He drew a deep breath and stepped inside.

Ella was asleep, her light-brown hair spread out over the white pillowcase, her face pale. Though she looked fragile, he knew she was strong. He admired her and had never stopped thinking about her over the years . . . as more than a family friend. As the woman he'd treated so badly . . . and the one he'd let get away. Not that there was anything he could or would do about that now. He still didn't trust his ability to commit. And Ella, with her painful past, needed someone who wouldn't bail on her again.

Seeing her in this bed brought him back to the time when they'd met. She'd been small for her age, a ten-year-old waiting to give bone marrow to her stepmother, much like Avery. Except Avery was giving her bone marrow to a half sister they'd known nothing about until a few weeks before.

Avery and Ella had bonded over their mutual situation, and all the Dare brothers had become extremely protective of Ella Shaw. It was what made his reaction to her that Christmas so damned . . . wrong. And why he'd treated her so badly afterward. Self-disgust turned at the wrong person. Because he'd enjoyed her hot, slick body too much.

He shook his head, pushing those thoughts aside.

He stepped farther into the room, and as he made his way toward her, those protective instincts he'd always had for her kicked in, combined with a healthy dose of desire for the woman lying helpless in the hospital bed.

"Excuse me. Who are you and what are you doing in here?" a female dressed in white, presumably a nurse, entered the room and asked.

"I'm here for Ella Shaw. I'm . . . family," he said, forcing out the words, because what he felt when he looked at her was anything but familial or brotherly.

The nurse narrowed her gaze. "Well, she's been through a trauma and—"

"It's okay, he can stay," Ella said, her voice raspy and low.

The nurse studied him for a long moment, finally treating him to a curt nod before rushing out of the room.

Tyler turned back to meet her gaze. "Hey, short stuff," he said, the nickname from when she was younger falling off his tongue.

"When I feel better, I am going to strangle Avery," she muttered. "I take it you're the cavalry?"

"You could sound more grateful."

"And you could speak to me like an adult," she snapped back, both falling into recent patterns.

To keep his distance and not show how attracted he was to her, he'd put up a wall, treating her like an annoyance or a pesky younger sister. That shit had to stop now. She was right. They were both adults, even if he hadn't been acting like one for the last few years.

He pulled up a chair, his knees touching the metal frame of the bed. "How are you?" he asked more gently.

She blew out a breath. "My head hurts badly, and I'm a little dizzy. Nothing out of the ordinary for a concussion," she said, eyes suspiciously damp, telling him she was in more pain than she let on.

Without overthinking, he reached for her hand. "I'm sure you'll feel better when we get you out of here."

"I was mugged. My money, passport . . . everything's gone."

"I know. But the good news is you don't need any of those things to fly out on a private jet."

The noise she made sounded more like a snort. An adorable snort but one nonetheless. "Of course not."

"Got a problem with that?"

"I wouldn't know. I've never flown that way before but . . . I'm grateful you came for me," she said, looking past him, toward the window, obviously unable to meet his gaze. "I'm sure you didn't want to and Avery had to twist your arm."

He squeezed her soft hand. "We'll talk about all that when you're stronger. Right now let's find a doctor who can release you."

It took a while. Finally, a harassed-looking man agreed she could leave as long as she had someone to watch over her. Since Tyler wasn't letting her out of his sight, that wouldn't be a problem.

The trip back to the hotel was more difficult, costing Tyler a fortune because, again, most cab drivers wanted to get home, not take passengers out of their way.

The palm trees swayed dangerously as they drove, the driver holding tight to the wheel of the small car.

Ella was oblivious. No sooner had he bundled her into the back of the cab than she'd curled up beside him, laid her head on his shoulder, and passed out. She might have been hospitalized, but she still smelled pure female. He hadn't thought anything could distract him from the fury of the hurricane, but one whiff of Ella's hair, an inhale of her scent, and he wasn't thinking about wind or rain. He was immersed in a force of nature of a whole different kind.

What kind of perv got an erection when a hurt, unconscious woman lay trustingly against him? Shit. The things this woman did to him always had him questioning his common sense.

When they reached the hotel, he woke her, and she leaned against him as they walked inside. He explained the situation to the desk clerk, who, thankfully, because of the photo shoot, remembered Ella and was willing to give her a key. With his hand on her back to steady her, they took the elevator up to the sixth floor, and she directed him to her room, 618, with a *Do Not Disturb* sign on the door.

"Wait. I didn't leave that on there," she said, pointing to the door hanger.

He narrowed his gaze. "Wait here."

He glanced around, but there was no safe alcove in which to hide her. He pushed her against the wall on the same side as the room in case someone came running out, then pulled out his gun.

Her eyes widened, but she didn't argue.

He slid the key into the door and let himself inside. The bathroom was immediately to the right, and he pushed open the door. Empty, as was the bathtub. The closet was on the left. He slid open the door. Also empty. He checked the balcony, which was still locked tight from the inside.

But the room had been ransacked, all her things tossed around. This unexpected turn of events told him the mugging probably hadn't been random. "Shit."

He stepped back only to find her waiting in the room, mouth open.

"Didn't I tell you to wait in the hall?" he asked, pissed she hadn't listened.

She frowned at him and stepped inside. "Why would some-one do this?" she asked, taking in the mess.

"That is a damned good question."

She bent down to pick up a piece of clothing.

"Don't touch!" he barked out, harsher than he intended.

"What? Why not?" She rose slowly to her feet.

"So when the cops here investigate, at least they'll see things exactly how we found them." Although with the hurricane coming, Tyler doubted anyone would have time for or care about a burglary.

A glance at Ella, who was pale and shaky, and Tyler knew that he, on the other hand, cared a lot.

Get *Dare to Take* now at your
local bookstore or buy online!

ABOUT THE AUTHOR

Carly Phillips is the *New York Times* and *USA Today* bestselling author of more than fifty sexy contemporary romance novels featuring hot men, strong women, and the emotionally compelling stories her readers have come to expect and love. Carly's career spans over a decade and a half with various New York publishing houses, and she is now an indie author who runs her own business and loves every exciting minute of her publishing journey. Carly is  happily married to her college sweetheart and is the mother of two nearly adult daughters and three crazy dogs (two wheaten terriers and one mutant Havanese) who star on her Facebook fan page and website. Carly loves social media and is always around to interact with her readers. You can find out more about Carly at www.carlyphillips.com.

Carly's Booklist by Series

Dare to Love Series
Book 1: *Dare to Love* (Ian & Riley)
Book 2: *Dare to Desire*
(Alex & Madison)
Book 3: *Dare to Touch*
(Olivia & Dylan)
Book 4: *Dare to Hold* (Scott & Meg)
Book 5: *Dare to Rock* (Avery & Grey)
Book 6: *Dare to Take* (Tyler & Ella)

NY Dares Series
Book 1: *Dare to Surrender*
(Gabe & Isabelle)
Book 2: *Dare to Submit*
(Decklan & Amanda)
Book 3: *Dare to Seduce*
(Max & Lucy)

*The NY Dares books are
more erotic/hotter books.

Serendipity Series
Serendipity
Destiny
Karma

Serendipity's Finest Series
Perfect Fit
Perfect Fling
Perfect Together

Serendipity Novellas
Fated
Hot Summer Nights
(Perfect Stranger)

Bachelor Blog Series
Kiss Me If You Can
Love Me If You Dare

Lucky Series
Lucky Charm
Lucky Streak
Lucky Break

Ty and Hunter Series
Cross My Heart
Sealed with a Kiss

Hot Zone Series
Hot Stuff
Hot Number
Hot Item
Hot Property

Costas Sisters Series
Summer Lovin'
Under the Boardwalk

Chandler Brothers Series
The Bachelor
The Playboy
The Heartbreaker

Stand-Alone Titles
Brazen
Seduce Me
Secret Fantasy
The Right Choice
Suddenly Love
Perfect Partners
Unexpected Chances
Worthy of Love

Keep up with Carly and her upcoming books:

Website:
www.carlyphillips.com

Sign up for blog and website updates:
www.carlyphillips.com/category/blog/

Sign up for Carly's newsletter:
www.carlyphillips.com/newsletter-sign-up

Carly on Facebook:
www.facebook.com/CarlyPhillipsFanPage

Carly on Twitter:
www.twitter.com/carlyphillips

Hang out at Carly's Corner—hot guys & giveaways!
smarturl.it/CarlysCornerFB